OTHER

Harlequin Romances

by DOROTHY CORK

BUTTERFLY
MONTANE

by

DOROTHY CORK

HARLEQUIN BOOKS   TORONTO
WINNIPEG

Original hard cover edition published in 1972
by Mills & Boon Limited, 17-19 Foley Street,
London W1A 1DR, England

© Dorothy Cork 1972

SBN 373-01692-1

Harlequin edition published June 1973

The Harlequin trade mark, consisting of the word
HARLEQUIN and the portrayal of a Harlequin, is registered
in the United States Patent Office and in the Canada Trade
Marks Office.

Printed in Canada

CHAPTER ONE

IT was a frightening, exciting country, Parma Drew thought, and she could hardly believe that she would soon be living at its very heart.

New Guinea! Staring down from the plane through a floor of floating white cloud, she caught tantalising glimpses of steep dark valleys, a tangle of jungle-covered mountains, and tiny native villages perched high on ridges, their round thatched roofs looking like minute brown toadstools. Where on earth the D.C. 3 was going to land she couldn't imagine, but there must be an airfield somewhere. Already the blue harbour and green, eucalypts-dotted hills of Port Moresby, where she had changed over from the Bird of Paradise jet to this much smaller aircraft, seemed to belong to another world. England didn't exist. Even Australia, that she had left behind her only this morning, seemed aeons away.

Parma thought of Alec Rivers waiting for her some-where in these jungle-covered highlands. Did he feel as excited as she did, now that they were about to meet again? Her dark eyes, large in her small pale face, burned as she thought of the love that had flared up between them so quickly a few short weeks ago in Sydney. She had not thought after he went that they would be meeting again so soon, though in every letter he wrote he had urged her to come to T.P.N.G. 'You simply must sample the life up here before you even think of finding yourself another job, Parma,' he had written. 'I absolutely insist!'

It was hardly a proposal of marriage, but all the same—perhaps because of the intensity of her own feelings—she read serious intentions into it. She knew they had a lot to learn about each other before they talked marriage—after all, they had known each other only three weeks!—but in her own heart she was fairly certain that Alec was the man for her. It was particularly wonderful because when she had left England she had thought she would never fall in love again. Her heart, she believed, had been irreparably broken when William Cunningham, the man she loved, had eloped with one of her best friends.

Yet she had fallen in love again amazingly quickly.

She had landed this job at a girls' school in Sydney only a week after she reached Australia. It was a temporary job, but so what? She needed a safe, secure harbour and it solved a lot of problems because she could live in. Secretary to the headmistress, Miss Webster—filling in for Miss Mooney who, after twenty years, had taken long leave and gone to Japan. There, on the second day of term—it was fantastic!—Parma had met Alec Rivers. He was an Agricultural Officer from New Guinea, spending a few weeks' holiday in Sydney, and he had travelled down in the jet from Moresby with the Barlow girls, Caroline and Rosalind, who were boarders at Miss Webster's school. Discovering that he had inadvertently made off with the two woollen ponchos he had been carrying for them, he had called in at the school next day.

'It was fate—we met,' he told Parma a few nights later as side by side they cruised along the Longe Boarde in a city restaurant, piling their plates with smorgasbord food, and unable to stop looking in each other's eyes, to touch each other's hands.

It had been a heavenly time, three whole weeks of bliss. Parma's spirits were still high when, at the end of it, he went back to the Government Station at Varmari in the Highlands. He had given her a ring—a wide silver band set with three square pavonine opals. It was a dress ring, he didn't pretend it was anything else, but to Parma it was a promise for the future. She knew they would meet again, that they had by no means

6

reached the end of the story.

She looked forward to his letters, and was solaced by his constant demand that she come to New Guinea. He was not, in all honesty, a particularly good letter writer, and Parma missed the physical charm of his personality, the warmth and excitement of his kisses.

When it became fairly certain that Miss Mooney would be back within a month, Parma set the wheels turning for her own departure, writing to Alec exuberantly. She obtained her entry permit and hoarded her money in a positively miserly way, for the air fare was going to reduce her savings to a drastically small amount. She even started taking the prescribed two anti-malarial tablets per week. Everything in fact was arranged except the actual date of her departure.

Then, unexpectedly, Miss Mooney decided to return a fortnight earlier. How Parma's heart had leapt! It did mean a little less money, but the waiting had seemed interminable and suddenly it was almost at an end. She booked her flight, wrote to Alec; Miss Mooney came back and in no time at all Alec was only twenty-four hours away.

And now—here she was!

Already the plane was coming down through thin drifts of cloud, and below, in a green valley that looked like velvet and was surrounded by dark crumpled mountains, she could see the clear sweep of a runway. There was the gleam of a river and the white rooftops of European-type houses showed up in scattered groups. Kundalufa! Suddenly she was madly excited. Alec would have come into the town to meet her—in a matter of minutes they would be together!

It took a quarter of an hour to convince her that he was not there.

As she left the plane she was bewildered by the sea of brown faces that surged forward, by the wide white smiles, the flash of beautiful teeth. All around was the fantastic spectacle of people dressed in little but shells

7

and feathers and beads, mingling with smart natives in conventional dress, with sun-tanned European men, with women in cotton dresses and huge sunglasses, carrying fascinating Buka baskets as handbags. She was so completely entranced that at first she hardly realised that she had not yet found Alec.

Then, when she had collected her luggage—she had been through Customs in Moresby—and emerged slightly dishevelled from the small airport building into the hot bright sunshine of late afternoon, she came to her senses and began to absorb the fact that she had not been met.

She stood on bright green grass looking about her hopefully, her pigskin case at her feet, while people surged past, talking, quarrelling, running, gesticulating, little children squealing—none of them taking the slightest notice of a twenty-year-old girl waiting all alone for someone who hadn't come. Above in a pale blue sky huge galleons of clouds moved magnificently, and Parma pushed back the shimmering dark hair that had fallen across her cheek. Her small pink tongue appeared, to lick at her upper lip, a habit she had when nervous or uncertain.

So Alec had not come. Well, all right, it was a fact and she must accept it. *Something* had happened that he wasn't here. Possibly he had not got her letter in time. Possibly he had not been able to get away from work. Maybe he had taken it for granted that she would make her own way to Varmari where he was stationed.

Yes, that must be it. Parma felt relieved. It was a working day, after all, and it was not as if he were meeting a wife—or even a fiancée!

She glanced about her hopefully. She needed help. The crowd was dispersing with remarkable speed and Parma singled out the most imposing-looking European male in sight. It was not hard, because he was a giant of a man, tall, broad, with thick wavy hair like dull gold—almost the colour of his skin. He wore a white shirt and light bamboo-coloured trousers and his tan shoes gleamed with a beautiful shine. She had noticed him before in the hangar—asking for his 'cargo' and being told by an English-speaking native, 'Yes, sir—I bring it!'

Parma picked up the pigskin case that had been a gift from Miss Webster and moved swiftly in his direction, wishing that he did not walk with such long and rapid strides that she had almost to run to keep pace with him. Fine beads of perspiration dewed on her upper lip when at last, to her relief, he came to a halt near a dusty buff-coloured station wagon.

She braced herself, pushed back her hair, and drew a deep breath.

'Excuse me——'

He turned quickly and stared at her and she raised her dark eyes. He was immensely tall and he made her feel like a small child. Parma smiled brightly. 'I wonder if you would kindly tell me how to get to Varmari.'

'*Varmari?*' He sounded totally incredulous. His eyes, she could see now as he stood close to her looking down at her in a kind of amazement, were a curious mixture of blue and green and amber, and his lashes, at variance with the dark glinting gold of his thick hair, were black and straight, though their tips were oddly gold. His chin was decided—even aggressive—his mouth mobile and sensuous, and his shoulders were dauntingly broad.

Those strangely disconcerting eyes travelled slowly and deliberately over Parma, first from the silky fall of her dark hair to her parted questioning lips, then over the trendy sleeveless dress of heavy blue cotton that she had crocheted herself and that now was too warm in the burning heat of the sun. They moved on to take in her slim nylon-clad legs and fashionable blue shoes and pigskin bag, and finally they came back to her face and he asked with a cryptic tilt to his dark eyebrows,

9

'Have you missed your contingent? Though surely Varmari's too way-out for even the wildest of fashion shots.'

'Fashion shots?' Parma was completely at a loss.

The eyes appraising her remained cold. 'You're not a model, then? Not tall enough, of course. We had them here a week or so ago—posing against our primitive setting in all their strictly city ritual finery ... You must be an anthropologist, then.' Now there was a glittering irony in his tone, though he made his absurd statement with immense and shattering gravity.

Parma wanted to laugh. What an extraordinary pronouncement! She must pass it on to Alec—when she saw him. She looked hard at the man standing so close to her to reassure herself that he wasn't insane, and he most certainly was not that. She had seldom seen a man who looked more alert and intelligent, despite his chilling unfriendliness. She shook her head, at a loss for words, and her tongue played nervously with her upper lip.

'No? That may be as well. To my certain knowledge there's already one anthropologist doing his stuff at Varmari—and staying in the guest house. A male.' He considered her seriously, head down, brow creased. 'So if you're not an anthropologist you would do well to discard any ideas of tripping off to Varmari. It's no place at all for a fastidious little tourist like yourself. You take my advice and be satisfied with Kundalufa and you'll be nice and safe.' He gave her a nod that was plainly of dismissal and turned towards his car.

Parma, more than a little annoyed that she had not received a sensible answer to her enquiry, persisted stubbornly.

'All the same, could you please tell me how to get to Varmari?'

He faced her again. 'No,' he said curtly. 'And it's extremely unlikely—in fact I would say it's beyond the bounds of possibility—that you could get there tonight. I shall be driving in that general direction in the morning, but this isn't hitch-hiking country, and you'—with a glance that raked her blue get-up and lingered on her pretty shoes—'don't look like any sort of a hitch-hiker. I suggest you stay in Kundalufa and have a talk with the tourist agent in the morning. You'll find it enlightening.'

That at least was a practical idea, though he hadn't offered it very civilly, and Parma nodded thoughtfully. 'Thank you. I'll do that.' Despite his rather brutal indifference—or even because of it—she smiled her gratitude, her wide mouth appealing, and she was taken by surprise when he said shortly, 'I'll give you a lift into town if you wish. Here, give me that bag of yours.'

Parma, a little stunned by such unexpected gallantry, handed it over with a murmur of thanks and climbed into the car. She thought she was a good judge of character and this man was to be trusted even if he didn't like the look of her, and was not inclined to be over-helpful to a 'fastidious little tourist'. He just doesn't like tourists, she thought to herself, and soon had her belief confirmed as he got the car moving and they left the airstrip.

'You know,' he told her disparagingly as she looked out interestedly at the high mountains that ringed the town, at the long grasses and bright flowers and the clumps of bamboo growing by the roadside, 'looking at a map and picking out a musical name or two is not the way to begin a successful sightseeing tour of any country. Least of all *this* country.'

Parma's fine dark eyebrows were lifted and she pulled down her upper lip comically.

'I'm not a sightseer,' she protested.

'No?' He was sceptical. 'In that model dress and with those flimsily shod feet? I've seen plenty of girls of your sort before. I know them back to front.'

Well, who was she to contradict?

'What makes you think I picked Varmari the way you said?' she asked interestedly.

'Why else *would* you pick Varmari?' he asked dryly.

There was a slight pause. Parma was bristling slightly at being thought such a featherbrain. She wondered if she should tell this man about Alec, and decided maybe the less she said the better. She pretty obviously wasn't going to impress him, so she stayed silent.

'You have that talk at the tourist office tomorrow,' he said presently, 'and I rather think you'll settle for some other name. And next time you leave home, do a little homework before you so much as step on the plane ... I'll drop you off at the Bird of Paradise Hotel. I'm staying there myself.'

'I might prefer some other hotel,' said Parma quickly and defensively, because she did not like being taken for a simpleton.

'There *is* no other hotel,' he informed her with a quirk of his mouth that annoyed her still further.

And that was the sum total of their conversation.

Except, as he deposited her in front of a two-storied white hotel that looked reasonably modern and smart, she said politely, 'Thank you for the lift, Mr——'

'Adams. Pierce Adams. Think nothing of it, Miss——'

'Drew. Parma Drew.'

He gave her the slightest of smiles that did not reach his eyes and then he turned away.

Parma thankfully saw no more of him. He was not in the dining room when she went down to dinner. Afterwards, she stepped briefly out into the darkness of the paved terrace at the side of the hotel, where orchids bloomed profusely in tubs and a wind whispered and the air was caressingly cool. Low cloud scudded across a moonless sky and she hugged her white stole around her bare shoulders and thought of Alec. 'I'll get to Varmari in spite of Mr Pierce Adams and all his high-handed ideas,' she promised herself.

She went to bed early and slept deeply. It had been a long day.

She was up bright and early in the morning. Her mind was full of happy possibilities. Alec would be there when she went down to breakfast—or there would be some message from him—or the tourist clerk would tell her there was a coach leaving for Varmari in the next hour . . .

None of these things happened.

She was eating her grapefruit alone at a small table in the airy dining room, with its wide windows looking on to tropical garden, when Pierce Adams came in. He gave her a nod and walked straight past her. Parma, whose smile had been wide and forgiving because she was in a happy humour, felt rebuffed. That was no way to treat a visitor to your country. There was no doubt in her mind that this *was* his country. He belonged here as surely as did the great towering mountains that ringed the wide green valley where Kundalufa lay; as surely as did those brown-faced smiling people she had seen yesterday, decked out in their feathers and grass aprons.

And now, she thought, deliberately schooling herself not to look around to see where he was sitting and whether or not he was breakfasting alone—now she would forget all about him.

She went down town straight after breakfast. Kundalufa was a very small town in spite of the fact that it was an administrative centre. There were a few tiny shops and two big ones—B.P.s and Steamships, which looked rather like supermarkets, and with no difficulty at all she located the tourist agency.

The clerk was a brown-skinned New Guinean, very polite, very helpful, but no, Varmari was not included in any trips they ran. In fact, there were no regular schedules for as far out as that. The usual thing was for a group of tourists to arrange their own itinerary—with a little official help—and to charter a plane or a bus. He smiled and offered her a brochure on the Highlands, his pink-tipped finger pointing out coloured photographs of native markets, of singsing gatherings, of beautiful isolated cloud-filled valleys. It took some minutes for Parma to convince him that she was not interested—not just yet—but at last she got away. Feeling somewhat sobered and thoughtful, she walked down the street in the shade of tall casuarinas, to the post office.

There she was relieved to find that at least she would be able to send a telegram to the Agricultural Officer at Varmari.

'In actual fact, he's not there right now,' the post-master offered casually as Parma, brow wrinkled above her small straight nose, worked out the wording for her message. She looked up, her dark eyes widening.

'Alec Rivers is doing a round of some of the western valleys—he's been away for a week or more.'

'Oh!' Parma's brow cleared. So he wouldn't have got her letter! That explained why he had not met her. 'Do you know when he'll be back?'

'No, there I can't help you. It could be tomorrow, it could be next week ... Still want to send your message?'

'No, thanks.' Parma crumpled her paper and walked slowly out into the sunshine. What was the use of tele-gramming, 'I am in Kundalufa. Please come and fetch me,' if she might have to wait for a week? In any case, Alec would receive her letter as soon as he came back to the station.

But now Parma was in something of a dilemma. Her finances weren't all that healthy—particularly with the hotel tariff as high as it was—and she had to hang on to enough to pay her return air fare to Sydney. She couldn't risk waiting a week. She would simply have to get to Varmari somehow. There, she was sure Alec would have teed up somewhere for her to stay. The Adams man had mentioned a guest house, and they

14

were never as expensive as hotels. Suddenly Parma began to walk fast. She had a brilliant idea! It might entail the sacrifice of a little pride, but what did that matter? She hadn't an inflated idea of her own importance. She didn't care—really—what Pierce Adams thought of her.

He was outside the Bird of Paradise Hotel when she arrived there, leaning against the door of his car and smoking a cigarette. She thanked her lucky stars that at least he hadn't gone. He looked as though he were waiting for someone. She saw there were a couple of bags stacked in the back of the station wagon and on the terrace of the hotel two women were talking. His eyes strayed in their direction as she approached and she wondered which of the two was his wife or his girl-friend—if so lofty a being *had* a wife or a girl-friend. They both looked somewhere about his age—middle thirties—and were well and prettily dressed in what was apparently accepted New Guinea style—unfussy cotton dresses, sandals, and no stockings. Parma made a note of it and wished she had worn a lighter dress and discarded her nylons.

She was certain Pierce Adams knew she was there. Her dress was an eye-catching orange and he had seen her in it in the hotel dining room earlier on. But he waited until she was almost upon him before he moved his head lazily and acknowledged her with nothing more than a lift of the eyebrows. Parma felt herself flush with annoyance, but she said cheerfully, 'Good morning, Mr Adams. I've just had that talk you suggested with the man at the tourist place.'

He couldn't have been less interested. He dropped his cigarette on the ground and pressed it out with his toe before he said indifferently, 'True?'

'Yes.' Parma hurried on before her courage ebbed. He was rather daunting. 'There's no coach going to Varmari right away and I thought that perhaps—since you're going that way—you might kindly give me a lift

15

as far as you're going.' Her voice trailed off into little more than a whisper. He was looking at her with pained amazement as if he simply didn't know what to make of her. Parma's chin tilted a little and her glance did not waver as she made an effort to appear sensible and composed, and to impress him that here—somehow—was a very reasonable request.

He said slowly, consideringly, 'I might even do that.' Hope sprang like a light into her eyes but faded away as he added crushingly, 'But no, Miss Drew—on second thoughts, definitely not. At the rate you're going, you're going to have it hard enough, and I don't wish to have a hand in it. You just do your sightseeing in the regular way or you'll find yourself in a lot of trouble. This is a wild country.'

'But—please——' Tears of frustration welled into her eyes and she turned her head slightly to hide them. And through those tears, swimmingly, she saw the name lettered largely on a pale green suitcase in the back of the car: H. Barlow. Her glance flew up. The Adams man had moved slightly and was looking over her head and asking pleasantly, 'Ready now, Helen?'

Helen. H. Barlow. The mother of Caroline and Rosalind? Parma's heart started an excited pounding. She turned to look at this Helen. The taller and slenderer of the two women who had talked on the terrace; sleek nut-brown hair, high cheekbones, fine lines about dark grey eyes. Something—surely—of the look of twelve-year-old Rosalind. Parma said with a rush:

'You're Mrs Barlow, aren't you?' She just had to take a punt. She knew it was no use waiting for Pierce Adams to introduce her. All *he* wanted was for her to go away—but quickly! 'I'm Parma Drew—and I know your daughters, Caroline and Rosalind.'

The older woman's surprised smile was utterly friendly—an unmistakable signal to Parma of rescue on the way. Mrs Barlow would see that Pierce Adams gave her that lift, and she quizzed him a little maliciously. Her eyes said, 'What can you do about *this*?'

He gave her a coldly narrow look and his mouth lifted cynically. He groped for cigarettes and occupied himself with them, leaving the field to her. He was pure spectator. He stood slightly away, but she was sure he was listening attentively to her performance.

Mrs Barlow, unaware of any hidden drama, had exclaimed, 'How extraordinary! You're from Sydney, then—and you're here on holiday?'

'Sort of,' said Parma cautiously. She would have to explain the situation briefly. But she would take one fence at a time. 'I was Miss Webster's secretary while Miss Mooney was in Japan. She's back now and—well, I'm on my way out to Varmari to see a friend, and I'm having a little difficulty getting there.'

'To *Varmari*?' It was the same incredulous reaction she had received from Pierce Adams yesterday, and she was aware of a quick glinting glance from him, sharp and sudden as the thrust of a knife. 'Who on earth——' Helen Barlow began, and then a curious expression crossed her face. She looked quickly at Pierce Adams and away again. She asked Parma tentatively, 'Would your—friend—possibly be the Agricultural Officer, Alec Rivers? He went down with the girls——'

Parma nodded quickly, excitedly, a tiny bit triumphant, and happy to be talking about Alec to someone who knew him. 'Yes, it's Alec. *They* forgot their ponchos—or Alec forgot he had them—*so* he brought them back to the school and *so* we met. And——' She nearly added, 'And so we fell in love,' but she bit off the words in time. All the same, the phrase seemed to hang upon the air and she finished rapidly, 'And now I've come to see him. But I've discovered he's been away from the station so he didn't get my letter, and that's why he didn't meet me. I want to be at Varmari when he gets back—and—and surprise him.'

'You might find you've surprised yourself even

17

more,' said Pierce Adams dryly. 'This girl,' he continued, turning to Helen, 'wants me to take her as far as Butterfly Montane. She has the idea that it will be quite a simple matter to pick up a lift the rest of the way.'

Butterfly Montane! Was that where he was going? And what did it mean? Helen Barlow was frowning, and Parma said impulsively, 'I know it will work out—I'm usually lucky.'

Still Helen Barlow frowned. 'Varmari's just a tiny Government station, dear. Are you sure Alec meant you to go there?'

Of course Parma was sure and she nodded vigorously. She saw them exchange a look and then the Adams man said brutally, 'You're being all sorts of a fool, if you only knew. You'll wait here at Kundalufa for Alec and let him stra'ghten things out.'

Parma said, quite simply, 'No.' Because for one thing, she was not going to have this man tell her what to do. And for another—she couldn't afford it. Not if it was going to be a week.

'You'll enjoy yourself in Kundalufa,' said Helen persuasively. 'There are lots of things to see and do.'

Pierce Adams' greenish eyes were mocking. He was all prepared to get into the car and leave her there. 'Your tactics have failed,' that derisive look, that half-turned back, seemed to say.

Parma said slowly, 'I *can't* stay in Kundalufa. It's too expensive. And I don't have any spare cash for sightseeing.'

'Oh dear!' Helen looked hopefully at Pierce Adams, but his shrug was hard and unrelenting. Quite clearly, Parma's predicament was not his concern, and the girl waited a tense minute. Then Helen said with sudden decision, 'You'd better come and stay with me for a day or two. We can't leave you here—and we certainly can't drop you off along the road.' She looked quizzically at Pierce Adams whose silence was full of dis-

18

approval and told him placatingly, 'It's really the only solution, Pierce, under the circumstances.'

'What's the point, Helen?' he said irritably. He spoke as though Parma were not there. 'If the girl is silly enough to come rushing up here expecting a good time, let her take the consequences. It's the only way to learn.'

'You're too hard, Pierce. She looks no more than a child.'

'Looks can be deceptive,' he said sceptically. 'But all right—have it your own way.' Suddenly, aloofly, he accepted the situation and took command. 'Settle your account, Miss Drew—I presume you have enough money to do that—and get your luggage out here. I want to be on my way.'

Parma had mixed feelings. She was grateful to Mrs Barlow, but she hated now accepting this favour from the Adams man, who was so ungracious. She would be thankful when she had seen the last of *him*!

Soon she was installed with her luggage in the back seat of the station wagon and they were leaving the town. Parma leaned forward to say, excluding Pierce Adams pointedly, 'This is terribly kind of you, Mrs Barlow. I really didn't mean to impose on you. I'm sure it will be only for a day or two.'

'We'll let them know at Varmari where you are,' Helen Barlow said cheerfully. 'But in actual fact, I'll enjoy having a house guest. I like company—I've been staying with friends in town the last few days. I miss my daughters and you can tell me about them. I'm sure you'll find it interesting at the plantation, too.'

'The plantation?'

'Yes. Pierce's coffee estate, the Butterfly Montane. My husband is overseer there.'

Parma drew in her breath sharply. She had not counted on this! She had thought she would be free of Mr Pierce Adams very soon. She comforted herself with the reflection that at all events it would be only a few days at the most. And in the meantime, who knew? She might yet get that lift on to Varmari. She would certainly keep her eyes open for a vehicle going that way.

After a time she caught him looking at her speculatively in the rear vision mirror. No, he didn't like her any more than she liked him. He thought she was scatterbrained, irresponsible, though that was surely not enough for such instant and positive dislike. She moved further into the corner, where he could not catch her eye, and looked through the window. They had left the town behind and were driving along a narrow dirt road that wound up and up, higher and higher into the mountains. Presently they passed a village of native houses clustered on a cleared slope high above the roadway. They were round houses, made of cane and bamboo, their peaked roofs a thick thatch of narrow grasses. Natives wearing aprons of string or grass were putting up the framework for a new house and further along in huge cultivated vegetable gardens, near-naked women weeded and dug, some with babies in net bags that hung down their backs.

Tall casuarinas stood out against the darker jungle, clumps of bamboo rustled. Above in the pale blue sky a procession of clouds floated, though the sun was burningly hot. Ahead, range after range of jungle-covered mountains stretched to infinity, their peaks disappearing into the clouds. Parma began to feel deep in her bones the strangeness and wildness of this primitive hidden land that had not known intruders from the outside world until the middle of the twentieth century. Gradually she began to see, too, the absurdity of her hope that she might pick up a lift to Varmari.

Imagine being set down here! So far, the only other vehicle they had met had been a red sports car coming from one of the coffee plantations whose dark trees spread over acres of rolling hillside high in the ranges. And of course, it was heading for Kundalufa. Then, as they rounded a wide curve in the road, a truck came rattling towards them at high speed. It was battered and dusty and it was crammed full of wild-looking natives wearing fearsome feather headdresses, and carrying huge black bows and bunches of arrows. Their faces were painted with red and yellow clay and they wore long bones through their noses. They were beating drums and shouting—or singing—at the tops of their voices and Parma knew an instant of pure terror.

Pierce, with a swift drag on the wheel, pulled the station wagon to the side of the road where it brushed through a wall of thick tall kunai grasses. The natives waved and shrieked and Parma was showered with fine dust. Too late she shifted away from the window and Pierce's eyes gleamed mockingly.

'There's nothing to be afraid of, Miss Drew. Just a truckload of high-spirited natives on their way to some celebration. It's not an uncommon sight.'

Parma managed a wavering smile and sank back in the seat. Her heart was hammering.

No, she reflected, feeling beaten and subdued, she could not possibly be set down somewhere along the road in the hope that she might pick up a lift. Pierce Adams was infuriatingly right, and she, Parma, was quite stupidly and indisputably wrong.

CHAPTER TWO

It was noon when at last they drove up the long narrow dirt road between the acres of coffee trees on the Butterfly Montane Estate. Feather floating shadows of the tall casuarinas that sheltered the coffee trees fell across the roadway and the sound of a gong sang and vibrated in the air. It had a magic sound to Parma, but Helen Barlow said matter-of-factly:

'*Belo*—break for lunch. We've timed it nicely, Pierce. David will soon be in.'

Parma moved in her seat. She longed to take a cooling shower and to change out of her dress. She wished that she had had the sense not to wear stockings and to wear cool sandals as Helen did. In fact, she was very conscious that she was not a Territorian. Her cheeks were warm, her hands felt sticky, and the strain of the journey into the hills had wearied her. Even the thought of Alec was too much just now—all she wanted was a shower, a light meal, and a rest in a cool shaded room. She was being escapist, of course. A dreamless sleep—and then to wake and find Alec had come to take her to Varmari away from Pierce Adams.

Whose dry uncomforting voice now broke in on her reflections.

'Respite, Miss Drew. We've arrived. If you take my advice, you'll eat lightly, shower, and retire to your room. You look done in already.'

'I'll look after her,' said Helen.

'I'm sure you will. I'm sure you'll hand her a big slice of comfort on a gold-edged plate, Helen.'

So what? thought Parma. It was nice to be made welcome, to be looked after when you came to a strange land. Suddenly she was more weary than she could have told. Reaction was setting in with a vengeance. Almost she wished she had stayed at Kundalufa despite the cost. She should have taken a chance that Alec would turn up in a day or two.

A bungalow had come into sight, flamboyant colours of exotic flowers dancing vibratingly about it in the heat. Oranges glowed from trees, a draught of heavy over-sweet perfume was wafted into the car. It was, thankfully, the Barlows' bungalow Parma didn't know and didn't care where Pierce Adams' house was. She was thankful to climb from his car, utter formal thanks, and follow Helen on to a fly-screened verandah and into a house that was dim and peaceful.

The front door opened straight into a sitting room that had an Indian-type rug in red and beige on the floor. There were low tables and a linen-covered couch and chairs. Bamboo-shaded windows looked across the verandah into the groves of dark-leaved coffee trees and their sheltering casuarinas. There was a distant prospect of white-wreathed mountain tops and pale blue sky where clouds suddenly swarmed and as suddenly disappeared.

Parma's room was furnished with a divan-type bed and a wardrobe that was more utilitarian than beautiful, but was more than made up for by the dazzling view from the window. A long narrow counter was built in along one wall and was backed by a mirror. It was all comforting, and, in a way, homely.

Helen's husband, David, came in to lunch and they met over cold pork and salad vegetables fresh from the garden. Parma knew Helen must have given an explanation of her presence and found David Barlow suave and quite charming. He was a slightly stocky sun-tanned man with a greying moustache and kind, keen blue eyes, and obviously he adored his wife and his daughters.

'Well, this is a surprise—and a pleasant one,' he admitted over lunch. 'I've been on my own these last few days and now I have two charming women to solace me! Helen will enjoy your company, Parma. May I call you that?'

'I'd like you to.' Parma helped herself to salad from the wooden bowl and passed it across to Helen. 'I suppose you think it an odd name, and I'm afraid I don't really know why I was given it, though I think it must have had something to do with Parma violets. I was orphaned at four, and I don't really remember my parents.'

'How sad for you!' Helen said sympathetically, and David said warmly, 'Be our daughter for a while, then.'

'Thank you.' Their kindness contrasted with Pierce Adams' inhospitality, and a slow flush mounted to her cheeks. 'It's wonderfully good of you, but I'm only staying here a day or so—till Alec comes.'

'Oh?' David Barlow sounded surprised. 'Helen tells me you were the headmistress's secretary at the school in Sydney. You look scarcely old enough to be more than a schoolgirl yourself. Did you know our daughters well?'

'Fairly well. I lived in, so I saw quite a lot of the boarders.' Her smile was happy and spontaneous. 'I loved it there, but it was only a temporary position. I used to do dormitory duty, to relieve Matron. I thought your girls were sweet.'

'Parma met Alec Rivers when he took something or other to the school for the girls, David. She's hoping to see something of him while she's in the Territory.'

That, thought Parma, was a bit of an understatement, but she let it pass, and David said, 'Indeed! Well, Alec is a man with more than his fair share of charm—or so I understand.'

Parma looked up and saw an odd look—a warning look?—pass to David Barlow from his wife. What did it mean? And hadn't she seen much the same look pass between Pierce Adams and Helen yesterday?

She said carefully, 'Actually, Mr Barlow, I was hoping for Alec to meet me and take me straight to Varmari, but my plans went astray. It was very kind of Mrs Barlow to allow me to come here.'

'Please call me Helen, Parma. You make me feel about a hundred when you call me Mrs Barlow ... And it's not just kindness to have you here. I shall love it.'

'My wife means that,' David Barlow said. 'Visitors are all too few. You must make yourself at home with us. You might like to go with Helen some time when she's collecting folk stories. I suppose she's told you all about that little hobby of hers already.'

Parma looked questioning. 'No.' Helen had said very little in the car—probably because she knew that the Adams man would put a dampener on any agreeable conversation.

'No? Well, Helen goes off now and again to some of the villages with her tape recorder and persuades some of the older natives to tell her folk stories in pidgin English. She's making a collection of them for a book, but I'm afraid that few of them get further than the tape. When it comes to writing them down in English, polishing them up, and then typing them out, she isn't making a great deal of progress. A typewriter is one of the few things my wife really can't handle.' He grinned amiably across the table and Helen smiled faintly.

She said gently, 'The folk tales wouldn't mean much to Parma, darling.' Then, changing the subject, 'Do you have to go out again this afternoon?'

'I do, my dear. Want to come?'

'I'd love to.'

'What about you, Parma? Would you like to have a look around the plantation? I'm going to supervise some pruning—I've a few new workers on this week.'

Parma said tactfully, 'If you don't mind, Mr Barlow——'

'David,' he corrected her.

'David,' she repeated shyly. 'I think I'd rather have a rest this afternoon.'

He gave her a searching look.

'You do look washed out. Well, have your rest. There'll be plenty of other days for you to see how we conduct our affairs at the Butterfly Montane.'

Parma didn't argue, but there wouldn't be all that many days—she hoped. She was certainly interested in the plantation, but she was even more interested in getting together with Alec again—and in getting as far away as she could from the inhospitable Pierce Adams.

Belo had summoned the men back to work a good half hour before she finally reached the shelter of her room, where she slipped into a short cover-up and prowled restlessly about. She was weary, but her mind was too busy to allow her to sleep. The house was empty now except for the *hausboi* Witni, and for a while she was conscious of the faint sounds of the dishes being dealt with. Then there was silence. Parma stood at her window looking out through banana palms and hibiscus trees and shrubs she did not know, flaunting bright fragile flowers. The garden was a tangle—a jungle—of prolific green. Beyond it she could glimpse the other bungalow, long, low, older-looking, with deep eaves that sheltered wide verandahs. It was hedged with citrus trees and palms and a variety of flowering shrubs and in the garden was a small cottage, to accommodate extra guests, she supposed.

She fell deep into a daydream as she stood there—a daydream in which she and Alec were married—living in a house like this one, with butterflies in the garden, mists wreathing the mountain tops beyond, the nights brilliant with starlight, throbbing with the sound of drums...

In the midst of it all she saw the Adams man appear in the garden behind his bungalow. There, red and orange canna flowers sent forth their blazing flags of colour, marigolds gleamed like little suns, and a tiny brown child wearing a minute grass skirt and a string of beads terminating in a white cowrie shell suddenl ran out happily, plump baby arms uplifted. Parma saw the planter stoop and lift her, swinging her high into the air so that she laughed down at him. Then he held her against his shoulder and strode out of Parma's sight.

Parma was shaken. She didn't know what it was that had shaken her. She was reasonably certain the child was not his—it would belong to some worker on the estate. But something—something—had shaken her. Perhaps it was because his actions had seemed so much out of character. She had thought him hard, cold, almost inhuman . . .

Restlessly, she threw herself down on the bed and sent her thoughts back to Alec.

But soon she was thinking of the planter again—seeing him now as the *Masta* who ruled—perhaps benevolently—these fertile acres of a primitive land where coffee trees now grew. Even as her eyes closed and she drifted into sleep she was disturbed by the memory of his eyes—unreadable, chameleon, hostile, summing her up—and dismissing her.

She thought it unlikely that they would see much of each other.

As it happened, they met again sooner than she expected.

Wakened later in the afternoon by the sound of *belo*, she rose quickly and took a shower. The house sounded empty still as she slipped into a white dress of fine cotton with a fragile black design. She tied a chiffon scarf of filmy peacock blue, that matched exactly her opal ring, at her slim waist and emerged hesitantly from her room. The *hausboi*, Witni, in neat shorts and khaki shirt came towards her.

'*Masta Adams i kam.*' His smile was wide, friendly.

'*Mi wokim tupela kopi. Yu savvy?*'

Parma listened intently, gravely. She didn't much like the sound of Masta Adams, but she got the idea that coffee was involved. There seemed no course open to her but to follow the *hausboi*, and as she moved, she heard the hiss of sudden rain on the hard ground outside. The sitting room was lit by an eerie light from a cloud-scudded sky that was pierced by the struggling rays of a red sun.

The planter rose from a chair near the window and a shaft of fiery red light blazed through the dark gold of his hair. His eyes were dark shadows that were unreadable, but Parma saw the curl of his lip as she appeared. It was the only greeting he gave in response to her smile.

The coffee tray was on a low table and the *hausboi* had gone discreetly away.

'You look rested, Miss Drew. I'm glad you took my advice. You weren't tempted to go and take a look around the plantation?'

The words implied a criticism of her and his eyes met hers as he crossed to the coffee table and poured two cups from the tall bronze-coloured coffee-pot. As though he owned the place, thought Parma, and wondered if he were in the habit of making himself so entirely at home in his overseer's bungalow. He handed her a cup and waited for her answer.

'I needed that sleep too much,' she said briefly. It was futile to bandy words with the Adams man. She took her coffee and found a chair—as far as possible from the one he had been using. But he followed her and stood looking down at her.

'You should be thankful that Alec Rivers is stationed in the Highlands. You wouldn't last long in the exhausting heat of the coast, I assure you ... Are you taking some anti-malarial prophylaxis, by the way? I hope to God you've had the sense to do that. We may not have mosquitoes in the mountains, but malaria's not unknown.'

'Don't worry. I'm taking Nivaquin tablets,' Parma assured him coolly. She sipped her coffee and looked at him warily through her lashes. His good looks, the forcefulness of his personality were overpowering and she wished she could like him She wished too that he had kept away from the bungalow if he had come here only to bait her. She was not accustomed to such hostility.

'I wonder why you're so determined to dislike me,' she asked curiously after a moment's silence during which nothing was to be heard but the beat of the rain on rooftop and ground. 'I've done nothing to hurt you——'

His eyebrows lifted a trifle. 'Let's make it a little less personal, shall we?' he asked on a drawl. 'It's not you in particular I dislike, Miss Drew. It's your kind in general. Young, sexually attractive, citified girls who come to the Territory without bothering to find out what it's all about. In rugged primitive country like this it should be a foregone conclusion that most of the usual luxuries and conveniences will be lacking. Yet you come here expecting the lot, and when you don't get it, you'll run away in disgust.'

'Shall I?' Now it was Parma who raised her eyebrows and she looked innocently around at the pleasant comfortable room, then towards the lovely tangle of rain-wet garden beyond the verandah. 'You mean I—and my kind—will run away from your plantation in disgust? You must be joking!'

'Now use your sense, Miss Drew.' His smile was faint but ironical. 'What woman these days is satisfied to live in a cage?'

'Helen Barlow,' suggested Parma, echoing his smile.

'Helen's exceptional. Moreover, she was brought up in the bush, which you very obviously weren't. However, when it comes to your case, my plantation doesn't really come into the picture, does it? Or'—one eye-

29

brow went up infuriatingly—'does it? Maybe you've changed your mind about looking up the Didirman at Varmari.'

'The——? I beg your pardon?'

'The Didirman—the Agricultural Officer,' he elucidated with a look of amusement. 'Alec Rivers.'

Her eyes widened and she returned his stare, throwing in a bit of amusement on her own behalf. 'Do you really imagine I might prefer to stay here—on *your* plantation, Mr Adams? I assure you I shall join Alec just as soon as it's possible.'

His strange gold-flecked eyes challenged her. 'We shall see about that when the time comes.'

Parma bit her lip to stop herself from arguing which she knew was pointless. He had made up his mind about her. She was a clueless, citified tourist ... She finished her coffee and the sharp rain that had been a continuous seething background to their conversation ceased suddenly, leaving a silence that vibrated.

Parma put her cup on the table and with sudden restlessness wandered across to the open window. The sweet scents of the garden, released by the rain, were almost tangible. She saw a blue and black butterfly poised over a flower—beautiful, jewel-like, its wings shimmering ...

'I suppose you've persuaded yourself you're in love with the Didirman and are looking forward to a high-powered romance.' The planter's voice came from close behind her.

'No, I haven't persuaded myself. It just happens to be a fact.' She could feel him standing behind her, very close. He laughed briefly and his breath stirred her hair. It was warm—human—too close. It made her clench her teeth, her fists.

'I'm afraid I'm not convinced. I don't suppose you even know what an Agricultural Officer does.'

'But I do,' said Parma obstinately. She scratched her mind frantically. She didn't really have much idea of what Alec did—they had been too busy falling in love with each other in Sydney to talk about such mundane things as work and everyday life! But wasn't that the whole idea of her coming here?—to learn all those other things about him she didn't know? She remembered a few odds and ends he had told her when they first met and she had asked him about New Guinea, and she felt a sense of triumph. She turned quickly and nearly lost her balance, the Adams man was so close to her. He caught her roughly by the arms so that she was pinned for a breathless instant against him, and her words came out in a panicky rush.

'Alec's—teaching the natives how to grow cash crops —how to raise cattle—so that they can earn money— and add protein to their diet——' Her voice faded away, she felt utterly helpless in his grasp and those strange eyes were so intent on her small pale face. 'They eat,' she almost whispered, 'mostly sweet potato —kaukau——' She could feel his breath close to her face, close to her lips, and suddenly she wrenched her arms away from him and stood trembling and straight, her upper lip caught between tongue and teeth. When she dared to look at him he was studying her unsmilingly. What was he trying to do? To prove that she was—looking for a high-powered romance? She didn't in the least doubt that he would be capable of providing it, but she had no use for games of love.

'You're very easily frightened,' he said dryly, but he didn't attempt to touch her. He moved easily away from her and lit one of his inevitable cigarettes, carelessly extending a silver cigarette case to her. She shook her head and watched him warily. She thought, 'He's used to women less conventional than I—women who are fierce and passionate and will demand his kisses rather than shrink away from them.' She remembered again the little brown child who had run to him so trustingly, and she wondered——

'You didn't do so badly,' he said after a moment of

smoking thoughtfully. 'You appear to have a rough and rudimentary knowledge of one or two things ... But I'm afraid you'll find the reality stark—as others before you have done. The Territory is tough—it's not a place you can play around with. It's a country that breeds tough characters, and you can only belong if you're prepared to be tough yourself.' His eyes smiled down at her, flicked over her pretty dress and her slender waist. 'In a week or two at the most you'll have discarded your pretty daydreams about the Didirman. I've seen it happen over and over again, it's a story repeated so often that one wearies of it. And that, Miss Drew, may give you some idea of why I don't go out of my way to encourage girls like you. You're made of sugar and spice and you'll melt in the rain.'

Abruptly he turned his back to her—a broad powerful back. Parma, whose cheeks were red, looked at it speculatively. Had that happened to him? Was that why he was so hard, so cynical? And had he—in despair of ever finding someone like Helen Barlow who would be happy here—had he—

She heard herself asking in a cold clear little voice, 'Are you—married, Mr Adams?'

'No, I am not. But that little fact needn't interest you, Miss Drew.' He faced her abruptly and his glance was cold as steel. 'Well, I've wasted enough of my time. Remind the Barlows when they come in, will you, that they're dining with me tonight. You'd better come along too.'

He had gone so quickly with long swift strides that he could not have heard her sharp angry retort. 'No, thanks. I'd rather not.'

Of course she went with David and Helen to dine with him. Politeness to the Barlows gave her no option. And at all events, she was curious—that she could not deny even to herself. She might hate Pierce Adams, yet there was something about him that fascinated her at the same time.

It was a strange evening. It was strange simply to walk through one garden in the blackness of a night whose airs were cool and caressing and enter the sweet-scented thickets of another similar—yet wilder, more jungle-like—garden where palm fronds whispered and the heavy velvety white heads of gardenias brushed against one's arms. Then up two steps on to the wide sheltered verandah of a long white bungalow to a screened door from which shone soft orange light.

A bachelor's house, plain and simple? Parma didn't really know what she expected. But soon, as they were welcomed inside by a suave smiling host, she was chiding herself for letting her always over-inventive imagination take over. Pierce Adams tonight wore dark trousers and immaculate white shirt with a silk cravat that gleamed green and blue like peacock's feathers and he seemed inclined to be perfectly affable.

Pierce Adams' house. The room into which they were shown was long and shadowy, lit by low orange shaded lamps. The blinds had not been drawn and wide windows showed the garden, gently illuminated by concealed lighting, red and orange flowers burning amidst the dark green foliage. But inside—inside Parma was aware of savagery. She felt it instantly. The walls were hung with *tapas*—long strips of beaten bark painted in strange primitive earth red and black designs whose significance she hadn't a hope of understanding. There were frightening fascinating masks, long and weirdly shadowed, carved out of wood, studded with shells and ornamented with red clay and twists of black hair. Human hair? A tall black bow and a grass tied bundle of fiercely tipped arrows were slung carelessly against a wall as if someone would use them very soon.

Parma, crossing the dark polished floor on to a thick rug of soft handwoven wool in stripes of natural, brown, and near-black, was completely overpowered by

33

the atmosphere of the room. It was oddly evocative of the man who lived here and whose eyes, glowing in the light from the coloured lamps, now seemed amusedly intent on her reactions. The crude—the primitive—the raw—they were all around. And yet, deep within her, Parma knew that this was, in a curious way, a very civilised room. Every native artifact, every bit of furniture—tables of dark wood, hand-made and with a rawness about them that verged on the sophisticated, couch and cushion coverings that echoed the underplayed tones of the rug—every object was chosen by someone who had an unerring, if unconventional, taste, an artist's eye.

Her inner preoccupation with the planter increased. She was sure that this room was all of his making. She could not imagine a woman who would create a setting like this. Certainly not Helen, whose house had a refinement and prettiness about it, a comforting homeliness. Parma was so caught up in an absorption of the atmosphere about her that she might not have been present for the first few minutes. She came back to herself almost with a start to find she had taken a comfortable bamboo chair with earth red cushions and that the *hausboi* was offering her a tray that held small stemmed glasses of sherry.

She took a glass of the pale liquid and smiled her thanks, and the *hausboi* smiled back at her. His black eyes were bright and friendly and he had the beautiful big perfect white teeth that seemed characteristic of the indigines. Two red hibiscus flowers were stuck in his hair, and he wore a white lap-lap edged in red, a well ironed red shirt, and soft-soled white sandals. She watched him continue on his way with the tray of drinks, heard Pierce Adams murmur a few words to him in soft-sounding pidgin English.

Then when he had gone—'Unkapenna wants to make a few additions to the dinner table before we go in—in honour of the *yangpela misis*! Enjoying your

34

sherry, Miss Drew?'

'It's very nice—quite as good as we get in Sydney,' she said with a slight smile, and saw his eyebrows go up humorously.

The *hausboi* announced dinner a few minutes later and Parma felt a shock of pleasure as they went through wide slatted double doors into an adjoining room. It was lit by three squat red candles on a long narrow table covered with a red cloth. Fruit—oranges, passion-fruit, a ripe pineapple, its spiky blue grey leaves so perfect as to look artificial—formed a centre-piece in an ancient black wooden taro bowl carved with a design of flying foxes, and down the centre of the table were tossed carelessly white hibiscus flowers with flame red centres and spikes of fragile white Hawaiian lilies that scented the air like incense.

'Mmm—candlelight!' exclaimed Helen in pleased surprise as they took their places, but Parma thought she sensed tension in the planter's face as he held her chair for her.

Pierce Adams poured a sharpish white wine, and Unkapenna served plates of delicious food—orange chicken with baked sweet potato and crisp french beans, very lightly cooked. Helen smiled across at Pierce, and told Parma, 'This is Unkapenna's speciality.' Parma found the meal irreproachable. A pink gecko moved silently across the ceiling as they ate, and Pierce and David talked plantation affairs. Parma listened absently, enjoying the food and puzzling a little over the planter, tonight so affable and tolerant even of her.

When the plates were removed and David had said an approving, '*Gutpela kai!*' the *hausboi* brought a light creamy passion-fruit dessert and plain wafer biscuits. Parma could not resist saying, 'Your *hausboi* is a wonderful cook, Mr Adams. Where did he learn such culinary art?'

She never received an answer to her question, for at

that instant there wafted into the room through the double doors the sweet notes of a clarinet playing the haunting melody, *Take My Lips*. A look of anger came into Pierce Adams' eyes and his nostrils whitened. He glared at the *hausboi* who stood smiling, waiting for approval, just inside the room, and Parma half expected to hear him snap, 'Turn that damned thing off!' Instead, his mouth grim, he rapped an abrupt, '*Maski!*' and turned his attention back to the dinner table.

But now his affability had gone. The sweet haunting music continued, but Parma seemed to be the only one enjoying it. Helen and David talked hard, and the planter talked hard too, but there was an angry set to his lips. Behind the clarinet Parma heard—or thought she heard—from out the darkness of the night, the throbbing beat of a *kundu* drum. The flickering flames of the candles made dancing lights and shadows in Pierce Adams' eyes and Parma could not keep her own eyes off him. Yet now when he glanced her way his eyes were hard and he made no effort at all to bring her into the conversation.

When they adjourned to the sitting room, he switched off the record player abruptly. His hands shook as he took out cigarettes and offered them around, and Parma had the feeling that he would just as soon the guests departed and left him alone. Most of all she had the impression that the animosity he was feeling was directed against her.

As they sat drinking their coffee and smoking in the soft lamplight, David Barlow remarked in his easygoing way, 'Helen tells me you saw the Gides in Kundalufa, Pierce. How are things at the Kunai Valley Estate?'

Pierce Adams shrugged his broad shoulders. 'They can hardly have improved. Arthur can't get even half the labour force he needs locally and of course he hasn't the money to recruit agreement workers from

36

elsewhere. It's a sad thing. Personally, I don't see any future for the estate unless he pockets his pride and accepts a bit of practical help from someone. The trees are in a shocking condition—they haven't been properly pruned for years. If I could take over the place for even a few weeks I could do something with it.'

David leaned forward to reach an ashtray. 'Well, you're about the only one Arthur converses with these days, and if he won't take help from you——' He made a gesture of dismissal. 'Trouble with these young fellows fresh out of agricultural college is they won't be told. Think they know the lot.'

'Now you know there's more to it than that, David,' Helen protested. 'Arthur's had a lot to contend with since he took over, and as Pierce says, his pride is involved. In a way, he's trying to cover up for his father.'

'Oh, come now, darling—it's common knowledge what went on out there. None of us holds that against him. It's that poor girl Sophie I'm most sorry for. She must wish she'd never come back here. What happened about the Didirman, by the way?'

Helen glanced quickly at Parma and said hurriedly, 'That fell through. Arthur just won't let *anyone* help. Isn't that so, Pierce?'

'It would seem to be so. But we're boring Miss Drew. I'm sure she doesn't want to hear talk she can't understand about other people's estates ... Have you any plans for tomorrow, Miss Drew?'

Parma shook her head. He was reminding her that she was a visitor, an outsider to be excluded from their talk. And she had been interested—particularly when David mentioned the Didirman—who must surely have been Alec. She wondered what it was all about and what Arthur Gide's father had done——

'Feel free to have a look around the plantation, then,' Pierce Adams said impersonally. 'And you might like to take a swim in the river—unless tiled pools are more to your taste.'

'I'm not used to tiled pools, Mr Adams,' said Parma quietly. 'I'm not used to luxury living at all.'

His eyes quizzed her coldly. 'Then that's fine. For you won't get it here.'

Parma, brought up in an orphanage, used, during her few weeks in Australia, to a small austere bedroom in a girls' boarding school, allowed herself a faint smile. This big sun-tanned self-assured planter knew nothing at all about her!

He said dryly, misinterpreting her smile, 'We're comfortable enough here. But of course Varmari is your objective.'

Parma was aware from a slight movement that Helen was ready to say they must be going, and she was thankful. Five minutes later they were all on the verandah on their way home when car lights made an arc in the dark and a four-wheel drive pulled up with a jerk beyond the garden.

Parma's heart leapt. If only it would be Alec!

CHAPTER THREE

At first she didn't recognise the tall man who came through the garden, his form lit by the light from the bungalow. He wore khaki shorts and an open-necked shirt, his dark hair fell untidily across his forehead, and his face was bearded.

The colour fled from her own face as she realised that it really was Alec. A strange feeling of panic took possession of her. He looked almost a stranger—so different from the suave clean-shaven man who had taken her dining and dancing and theatre-going in Sydney only a few brief weeks ago.

Another moment, and he had taken her hands in his, and yet she was holding back, hoping that he would not kiss her—not yet—not until she was certain it really was Alec.

'Well, what a surprise,' he said, 'to get back to the station and hear that you were in the Territory, Parma! I never imagined you'd arrange it all so quickly.'

Parma was aware that the others were listening, and wished futilely that they could have had their first meeting privately. She was particularly conscious of the planter's sardonic regard. She heard her own voice trilling nervously, 'Oh, Alec!—you look so different! You've grown a beard——'

'You'll soon get used to that,' Helen said with a laugh. 'Alec has a beard more often than not—he only shaves it off when he's going to *very* civilised places.' She linked her arm through David's. 'We're on our way home, Alec. Are you coming?'

'Yes, of course. Sorry to turn up so late, but it was now or God knows when.'

Parma's head spun. Somehow, although she had

longed for him to come, his arrival had taken her completely by surprise, and now he looked nothing like the man she had fallen in love with. She felt at a loss for words—at a loss for everything. And while she had had her wish—while he had not kissed her in front of them all—perversely now she wished that he had. So that Pierce Adams would know——

At last they got themselves away from the planter's bungalow. Parma had kept her eyes from meeting his, had said an almost childish thank-you for the dinner, for the lovely evening, and in minutes they were back in the normal undisturbing setting of the Barlows' sitting room.

David, all hospitality, brought whisky and iced water. Helen said she would make coffee, and Parma sat in a light that seemed over-bright, looking at Alec warily from under her lashes.

'A terrific piece of good luck for you to have run into Helen,' he told her presently, raising his whisky glass with a 'Cheers!' David had tactfully gone to give his wife a hand in the kitchen, leaving them alone. 'I was picturing you tucked away at the Bird, twice the distance away, till Helen's message came through on the evening sched.'

'But, Alec, I'm only here temporarily. I'll—I'll come to Varmari, of course, now that you're here.'

He stared at her, astonishment in his dark brown eyes. 'Afraid that won't be possible, honey. For one thing, there's a male anthropologist in the guest house already.'

Parma looked at him quickly. 'But why should that stop me from staying at the guest house too? Is there something particularly frightful about male anthropologists? I mean, do they carry on such frightful activities that——'

Alec, who had finished his whisky, set down the glass and explained carefully, 'It's not the sort of guest house you're thinking of, Parma. This is just a little bush house—thatched, one room—behind the Medical Officer's house. Even if it weren't occupied, a girl like you wouldn't want to stay there. The set-up is pretty basic—well, let's call it primitive. Besides which, there'd be nothing for you to do all day. You're better off here, believe me. You'll get on well with the Barlows. They like visitors and they're nice people.'

'Yes, of course, they're very nice,' agreed Parma helplessly. 'But I can't impose on them indefinitely.' She was finding it very hard to accept what he was telling her. She had been so certain that she would go to Varmari. She had made no bones about it when she had talked to the Adams man. Now, was he to have the last laugh? She bit her lip as Helen came in with the coffee tray.

'David and I are off to bed—we'll leave you two to talk,' she said cheerfully. 'I'll see you in the morning, Parma. Be good, Alec.' She gave them both a bright smile and was gone.

Alec came and sat on the couch beside Parma. He put his arm around her.

'Stop looking as though someone's taken your candy away from you, honey. I honestly hadn't a notion you expected to come to Varmari. I thought you knew it was just a little government station.' He tilted her chin with one finger and kissed her lips, wooingly, softly. And suddenly, in spite of his changed appearance, he was more the Alec she had known before and her heart began to melt, the knots that had tied themselves so tightly in her head they were giving her a headache began to unloose. Alec said softly, 'Varmari's deadly dull. There's a patrol officer, the med. officer and his wife—she's the postmistress too—this appalling anthropologist, Doug something-or-other—and me. The whole male contingent is away five days a week and you'd be on your own with Mrs Peters, who's about fifty, one or two natives who speak a bit of pidgin, and a few little brown kids.' He kissed her

41

again, and his brown eyes looked lovingly into hers and all his remembered charm seemed to come back and work on her once more. She relaxed against his shoulder with a sigh and let him take her hand in his.

'What am I to do, then? I came to see *you*, Alec.'

'We'll have the weekends,' he said consolingly.

'That's not enough!'

He laughed softly. 'Are you trying to seduce me?'

Her cheeks flamed. 'Of course I'm not, Alec.'

'I was teasing.' He kissed her fingers. 'You're wearing my ring. It's pretty—almost as pretty as you. And you look delectable. You always did. Don't tell me you made that dress with your own cunning little fingers—though knowing you I expect you did. It looks like it cost a hundred dollars.'

'It cost ten—for the material. And I did make it myself.' She stopped him from kissing her again to say, 'Alec, I can't just stay here. Helen asked me to come while I was waiting for you. And you see, I can't afford to stay in the hotel at Kundalufa. I haven't enough savings. I thought——'

'Well then, stay here. You can, you know. I've told you the Barlows love visitors. It will work out fine.'

'But it makes me feel like an opportunist.' She thought of Pierce Adams. *He* would think she was an opportunist—taking the easy way out, settling for something closer to civilisation. He was really the main reason why she had wanted to get away from the Butterfly Montane, as soon as Alec came.

'Forget about opportunists. You're in the Territory now. We don't think that way—we're hospitable.'

Not Pierce Adams, she thought. He'd have left her to sweat it out at the Bird ... She said, 'The coffee's getting cold.'

'Blow the coffee,' said Alec. 'So long as *you*'re not getting cold.' He pulled her into his arms and kissed her again.

Now her face was warm from his kisses and she felt loved—wanted. All the same, after a moment she drew away from him, handed him his cup of coffee, and started drinking her own. She said with a frown, 'If I could be *useful* in some way it wouldn't be so bad. And if I'm only to see you on the weekends, I shall have to find something to do.'

'Oh, you'll have a good time,' he said easily. 'Besides, if you're as close as this I'll be able to get over some nights.'

Parma, deep in her thoughts, had a sudden idea that made her brighten. 'Mr Barlow—David—said Helen has been recording some folk tales. I could get them typed out for her, couldn't I? Do you think that's a good idea, Alec?'

'I think it's a marvellous idea, honey,' he said comfortingly. 'But don't sit up so straight and so far away. Come closer.'

Presently he said, his voice near her ear, 'That's all settled, then. How long are you staying, by the way?'

Parma blinked. Didn't he knew that depended on him? 'How long would you like me to stay, Alec?'

'It's entirely up to you. We'll do our best to see you have a good time.' We? thought Parma, a little frantically. 'I'll pick you up this Saturday for a start and we'll spend the day together. Sorry there are no night clubs.'

'I don't mind in the least, Alec. I'll look forward to it,' she said slowly. She wished he would say, 'I love you', or 'I want you to like this country where I belong'. But she was being foolish, wanting too much too soon. They had to get used to each other again, had to make sure their attraction was lasting, could stand up to this different setting, this land that Alec had adopted as his own.

She said, before he went, 'The only thing I don't like about staying here is—Pierce Adams.'

'Has he been making a pass at you?'

Parma almost giggled. 'On the contrary. He can't stand me—nor I him.'

'It can't be as bad as that, surely.'

'I think it is. Do you get along with him, Alec?'

'Of course I do. It pays to be on good terms with Pierce Adams. He's the big man around here. I can't say I like him particularly—he's too interfering by half. But it wouldn't do to have a confrontation with him—not worth it. I'd advise you to stay on his good side, Parma. Just be tolerant and keep out of his way.'

'I shall,' she promised. Everything seemed easy now, and she was lulled and comforted by the feeling that Alec was on her side. His goodnight kiss when she went out to the car with him was only spoilt by the fact that when she turned back to the bungalow, she was aware Pierce Adams was somewhere in the offing. She could smell the peculiar fragrance of the tobacco he smoked, and wondered if he had witnessed that goodnight kiss.

The following day she learned something of the routine of the plantation.

She was wakened from a deep and restful sleep by *belo*. It was about six o'clock and full light. Parma heard soft movements in the bungalow as she lay listening drowsily, and presently she went to sleep again. Then an hour or so later the resonance of the gong roused her once again, and this time she rose. She slipped into her cover-up and left her room. Helen Barlow, already dressed, was in the kitchen and gave the girl a warm welcoming smile.

'Sorry about the morning noises. You'll learn to sleep through them in time. Want some coffee, or are you tired of it? There's tea if you prefer it.'

'Coffee will be fine, thanks.'

Soon Parma was sitting at a small breakfast table in the kitchen and Helen was explaining the day's procedure. First *belo* was to summon the men who lived on the estate to breakfast. At second *belo*, all the workers, including those who came from nearby villages, assembled and David, and often Pierce as well, joined them to delegate the tasks for the day. They also listened to any complaints, heard any requests, and saw if any medical attention was required.

'Pierce and I usually attend to the medical side,' Helen said. 'Minor injuries, or fevers, or sores, etcetera. I keep an eye on the women and children in particular. We only have a few families living at the plantation, most of them are local and come in from their villages. Pierce is very well liked by the indigenes and it's seldom the men fail to turn up without a very good reason. Butterfly Montane has the best reputation among the natives of all the coffee plantations in this district. We're never short of labour and don't need to tie anyone down for two years or take them away from their families.'

Parma listened with interest as she ate her breakfast. Somewhere on the estate a half hour or so later she could hear the men singing as they went to work—to prune, to weed, to clear. Or to harvest the ripe coffee cherries.

She showered and dressed quickly knowing that she must talk to Helen about future arrangements and feeling a little nervous about it. The *hausboi* Witni was doing various jobs in the bungalow, and Helen was in the garden cutting flowers. Parma went to join her there, a slight frown on her small face.

'Now what's worrying you, Parma?' Helen asked at once. 'Is there something wrong?'

'Not really. But I talked to Alec last night, and Mr Adams was right. I shan't be able to stay at Varmari.'

'Oh, I knew that,' said Helen easily. She held out the flat native-made baskets of gardenias towards Parma. 'Gorgeous, aren't they? ... Don't you worry about a thing, my dear. You're most welcome to stay with us.'

'I don't know what to say. It's too good of you—

45

when you didn't even know me. I hope I can do something in return.'

'Never mind about that. All you have to do is enjoy yourself.'

'I'm sure I shall, but I was thinking of your folk tales. I'm a typist, you know. Couldn't I type them out for you?'

'Now there's an idea!' Helen smiled. 'David would definitely approve of that. All right, we'll keep it in mind. When are you seeing Alec again?'

'He's coming for me on Saturday and we'll spend the day together. He said he may manage to call in one evening, too, in the meantime.'

'Wonderful! What about coming down to the river with me today? We shan't start work just yet. We've a lovely swimming spot a couple of miles away, and it's just the day for it.'

This suited Parma perfectly. It would get her out of Pierce Adams' way, for she had no idea whether he went around the plantation with his overseer or if he led a life of leisure at the bungalow.

Later in the morning they set off in Helen's car, and left it in a clearing off the narrow dirt road. They made their way down to the river through a tangle of trees and ferns and palms and brilliantly flowered shrubs. Parma could hear the mountain river as it rushed and tumbled and sang before they came through the trees to the picnic spot. There was a small curve of pebbly beach near a deep pool where the brown river widened. It looked remote, beautiful, idyllic beyond words.

They changed into their swim suits in the shelter of tall bamboo clumps and soon were splashing and swimming in the water where the current was curbed by a scattering of boulders that spread across the river's width. They were smooth grey-green boulders and made excellent bases to lie and sunbake or eat the picnic lunch that Helen had brought. On either side of the river, the jungle rolled back into swiftly rising hills. Outlined against the delicately blue sky were dark mountain tops, their heads hidden in cloud. The sun was hot, the water sparkled and murmured, and time passed like a dream

As they lounged in the sun the subject of last night's dinner came up, and Parma said musingly face down on the sunwarmed rock. 'That *hausboi* of Pierce's—Unkapenna—is a terrific cook. Where on earth did he learn?'

Helen flung back her nut brown hair and laughed. She was slimly built and had a youthful figure that looked well in the bright red one-piece swimming costume

'Yes, he's a marvel, isn't he? I wish I could teach Witni a few tricks. To tell the truth, Unkapenna has only two party dishes. That was one—chicken *à l'orange*. He can also do a very good roast stuffed chicken with bacon rolls.'

'But who taught him?' Parma, still curious, turned on her side to look at Helen.

The answer was brief, almost reluctant.

'A girl who stayed here once. Rowena Arnold.'

Of course it was not her business, but for some reason Parma persisted. 'One of Pierce Adams' girl-friends?'

The older woman, one foot dangling in the brown water below, hesitated. Then with a sigh, 'I might as well tell you. It may help you to understand Pierce better. Rowena was the girl he was going to marry. He was quite insanely in love with her and she was a sweet girl—dark-haired like you, with a very fair skin and a sort of—unworldly look about her that was, I suppose, quite misleading, for as it happened she put a high value on material things. She spent several weeks here, sleeping in the little *rum slip* in Pierce's garden and eating with him at the bungalow. We all liked her and Pierce was very happy.'

She paused, and Parma said, 'What happened?' expecting to hear of some tragedy.

But Helen shrugged lightly and said, 'One day—just a week before they were to have been married, to be precise—Rowena simply packed up her things and went back to Melbourne.'

'But *why*?' Subconsciously, Parma knew that to have been singled out by Pierce Adams—to have the chance to live here in these beautiful mountains—was one chance in a million. And to have thrown it away——

Helen gave her a wry look. 'She was very young—no older than you. It was a big step to take, to leave her home, and her family—who were very wealthy people, by the way, and I suppose indulgent. I think Rowena found there just wasn't enough to hold her here. There are a great many things that one has to do without, you know.'

'Do *you* mind that?'

'Oh no. I'm happy here,' said Helen off-handedly. 'But then I've never known the sophistication of city life. I was brought up on a cattle station in South Australia. I met David in Adelaide at a friend's house when both of us were holidaying there.'

'Just as I met Alec when he was on holiday,' thought Parma, her eyes narrowed against the glare from the water.

'But if this girl—Rowena—*loved* Pierce, wouldn't she have been happy here?'

'Ah, there's a question! I'm afraid I can't answer it. It's a question that every girl must answer for herself when she falls in love. Maybe her answer tells her how deep her love is—and what is most important to her in life. Perhaps Rowena was wise to go and would have ruined two lives had she stayed. But it's left Pierce with a scar that's taking a long time to heal, and has given him—what shall I say?—a complex about outsiders—girls from the city in particular——'

'Girls like me,' said Parma wryly. She sat up and stared pensively over the brown flowing water that glinted in the afternoon sun. So that was it. Pierce had been badly hurt—his heart—his pride too. She felt sorry for him, but she thought it unfair to take it out on innocent people—people like herself. Unfair to prejudge. She wasn't just a 'girl from the city'. There was a lot more to her than that. And she was certain he thought her used to far more sophisticated living than was the case.

Ah well, it didn't matter really. She stood up in her yellow two-piece swim-suit and tossed back her loose dark hair, seeing it capture blue and green lights from the sun. 'I'm going in again. Are you coming?'

'No, I think I'll get dressed. I've had enough. But you go ahead, Parma.'

Parma splashed and swam, watched a butterfly winging over the water. Her dark eyes followed it. Papillon, the butterfly of love. She had been chasing it in vain up till now. But now that Alec was back—— She plunged under the water in a sudden access of high spirits, and emerged spluttering, her hair clinging to her face and shoulders. Helen stood on the bank laughing at her, and she knew she was being childish.

She clambered out of the water and sat on a rock, rubbing her hair vigorously with her orange surf towel.

'Ready to come home in a few minutes?'

But Parma had not had enough. She was enchanted with this spot. 'Couldn't we walk along the jungle paths? It's all so beautiful.'

'I have to get back. I have the dinner to cook— Witni just doesn't seem to learn. But you stay if you want. You can find your way back, can't you? And you'll be perfectly safe down here.'

'I should come back with you and give you a hand.'

'Rubbish. I'll let you get dinner on your own one evening.'

'If that's a promise,' said Parma gaily, 'then I shall stay.'

49

'I'll see you later, then. Better start for home when you hear *belo*.'

'I'll do that.'

When Helen had gone. Parma decided against dressing at once and taking a walk. The water was so pretty and tempting she knew she would go in again Meanwhile she paddled upstream in the shallows, enjoying the pull of the limpid current against her legs. She wondered where Alec was today and if he would take her to see the station at Varmari on Saturday. She longed to see where he was quartered and to see for herself if it was too primitive for her. She would not be like that girl of Pierce Adams' who had measured life at the plantation against city life and made her decision accordingly. Parma thought she could not have been really in love. It was a pity that she should have had the power to sour Pierce's life for him. She thought of the unexpected tenderness he had displayed when he picked up that little brown girl. He was a man who should have children of his own.

Presently she perched on a boulder a few yards out in the river—a sprite of a girl in her scanty two-piece swim-suit, her dark hair falling against her cheeks, her thin arms clasped around one knee, one foot dangling in the water. In the light of her new knowledge she looked back on the dinner party at the planter's last night. She remembered Unkapenna's smile of approval as he offered her the sherry, his beaming face when he appeared at the door after setting that record going. That sweet beautiful clarinet weeping out the old melody of *Take My Lips*. She remembered Pierce Adams' tensed up look, his sudden withdrawal. Had it all been a scene re-enacted? Had that particular record been played when he was deep in a happy love affair with the girl from Melbourne? But why had the *hausboi* acted as he had? Was it because Parma too was young and dark-haired, and had reminded him of his *Masta*'s ex-fiancée?

Parma sat still as a statue, deep in her reflections, carried away by the power of her own imagination. She was convinced that she had made a valid interpretation of last night's happenings.

A sudden sharp splashing, breaking into the murmuring song of the brown mountain river, startled her back into awareness. She saw a man swimming down towards her with strong slow strokes. She saw his dark gold hair, his powerful brown arms, and the colour drained from her face. It was Pierce Adams. 'And he hates me for what I represent to him,' she thought. 'He hates me even doubly, because I remind him of Rowena Arnold.' She didn't altogether blame him, but it didn't make it any easier to bear. She stayed where she was, though he must have seen her, for he was heading straight for her.

In a moment he hauled himself out of the water and sat dripping beside her, smiling mockingly into her eyes.

'Well, Miss Drew, so you're still with us! I thought you'd have been off to Varmari. What's the hold-up?'

She stiffened, and wished that she had gone with Helen after all—or at the very least, that she had got back into her cotton shift. Because those eyes of his, more golden now than any other colour in the reflected light from the brown river, were making no pretence of not giving her a very thorough overhaul indeed. She was acutely conscious of her slight figure so fully revealed by the little yellow bikini. Her limbs seemed white and naked, and all she could do was to sit there and feel herself tensing as his eyes took her in at their leisure.

'What's the matter? You weren't so inarticulate yesterday.'

'I—I don't like to be stared at, Mr Adams.'

There was a little stunned silence and then he laughed harshly. 'Come now, you must know it's no novelty to see a woman's naked body in these parts.

51

And you're really very modestly covered, Miss Drew. Imagine if you'd just been wearing a bit of grass and a string of girigiri shells——'

She caught her breath and turned her head away, feeling deep colour stain her cheeks. Her tongue came out to lick her top lip and close to her ear he repeated his first question. 'How is it you haven't let the Didir-man carry you off to Varmari?'

'You told me yourself,' she said stiffly. 'There's someone else already in the guest house.'

'Is that all it is? Ah well, when the anthropologist's gone, I suppose you'll be moving in.'

'Yes, I suppose I shall.' Unwillingly she turned her head again and caught a stunning glimpse of his brown torso gleaming with water, of those eyes, savage in their intensity, that would not leave her alone.

'We shall have to make the most of your stay at the plantation then.'

'I assure you, I don't mean to bother you, Mr Adams,' she said huskily. 'I'm perfectly capable of amusing myself and—and——'

'Not afraid to stay here by the river alone? Now I'd have staked my soul that you'd have stuck close to Mother Helen. Or did she tell you I come down here for a swim most afternoons?'

'No, she did not. If I'd known, I most certainly wouldn't have stayed.'

His eyebrows went up. 'You're afraid of me, then?'

'I'm not afraid of you. But I don't like you. You haven't given me much reason to, have you?' Her voice shook a little, though she stared at him boldly. She swung her legs around ready to slip into the water and escape, but somehow she slipped and fell with a splash. When she surfaced, the Adams man was reaching down a hand to her, and in her state of shock she grasped it and let him haul her up beside him once more. He didn't let go of her hand. He pulled her close against him, and her body, shivering and wet, was pressed against his sunwarmed chest.

'I've saved your life I think that rates a kiss,' he said, his eyes gleaming. He bent his head to hers and kissed her lips. She submitted because his grip was like iron but she kept her lips tightly closed and didn't respond. It was punishment for Rowena Arnold and her kind. Nothing more, she was certain of it. When he let her go she wiped her mouth hard on the back of her hand and saw his lip curl.

'Not romantic enough? Well, you'll find other things besides kisses in a scented garden in this savage land, I promise you. Maybe you'll be prepared for danger another time.'

'There will be no next time for—for you,' Parma breathed. She felt sick and shaken.

'No?' He quirked his dark brows. 'You must learn to call me Pierce, by the way, seeing you're now a guest on my estate.' He stressed the possessive pronoun slightly. 'But believe me, I'm only offering you some of the heady romance you're no doubt hoping to find in the Territory. You're going to find life pretty dull between the Didirman's visits if you rule me out.'

'Then it can be dull for me,' said Parma, 'because I do rule you out.'

'Why?'

'Why do you think, Mr Adams?'

His brow wrinkled. 'I have no idea. You must tell me.'

'Because I find you—insufferable.' This time Parma managed to clamber to her feet successfully and plunge into the water, and in a minute she had reached the safety of the bank.

In the shelter of the bamboo clump she pulled her cotton shift over her head with hands that shook; dried her feet and slipped on her sandals. She was raking a comb through her wet hair when he appeared again.

The soft vibrating notes of *belo* sounded through

53

the sunny air as he stood looking down at her, kneeling in the long grass. Water dripped from his bare brown chest, from the dark gold of his hair. Hung glittering on his dark gold-tipped eyelashes. The expression in his eyes was unfathomable. Parma half expected him to drag her to her feet and her eyes were wide and frightened.

But all he said was, 'Wait a few minutes while I dress, Miss Drew, and then I'll drive you home.'

'*Maski*,' she said, her voice low. 'I'll walk.' She stared up at him and saw him shrug.

'Please yourself.'

Parma climbed back through the trees and started to walk along the road.

Halfway, she heard his car coming along behind and she moved well to the side of the narrow road. She really would welcome a ride back to the plantation, but she didn't turn her head. She simply walked steadily on—the epitome of the tough outdoor Territorian, she thought wryly to herself, wondering why she should be so intent on impressing him.

Now the car was level with her, was almost stationary. Pierce Adams leaned out.

'By the way, if you're meeting your Didirman on Saturday tell him we're having a picnic at the river pool. See how he feels about bringing you along to join in the fun. Tell him Sophie and Arthur Gide will be there.'

He gave her a nod and drove on.

Parma stared after him disbelievingly. 'Hateful man!' she fumed to herself. Her face was moist with perspiration and there was a film of dust in the air. She simply couldn't believe he had done this to her. The sun was burning hot and her sandals were making her feet sore.

She trudged on.

CHAPTER FOUR

PARMA didn't see Alec during the week after all, and Saturday, that she had looked forward to so much, was not by any means an unmitigated success for one reason and another.

Alec didn't arrive till after the others had gone down to the river, but he agreed that it would be a fine idea to join the picnic. It was not until they were well on their way that he asked casually, 'Who's down there?'

'The Barlows—and Pierce Adams. And some people called Gide.'

She saw his lips compress, but he drove steadily on. They reached the little clearing where the other cars were parked, but Alec didn't slow down. Parma said, 'You've passed it, Alec.'

'I've changed my mind,' Alec said. 'I want you to myself.' He turned his head to give her a quick smile, reached over and squeezed her hand. 'Do you mind?'

'Of course not.' She should have been happy at the prospect of a day alone with Alec—relieved that she did not have to put up with the planter, and yet—— She didn't know why she felt vaguely uneasy. She glanced at the man beside her in the car. He was still something of a stranger with his dark beard and his hair, that in Sydney had been so well groomed even though it was fashionably long, now looking rather untidy.

'Who issued the invitations?' he asked presently.

'Pierce Adams.'

'Hmm. Why can't he mind his own business?'

Parma wondered that too.

They drove another five miles and reached a swimming spot that Alec knew. It was not so pretty as the other pool. The banks were grassy, but the trees did not grow so thickly, and the water was too swift for Parma's liking. She soon left Alec to amuse himself in the deep water and satisfied herself with the shallows near the bank.

She had brought a small picnic basket with her at Helen's insistence—'just in case' Alec decided not to join the others. But it was not a terribly successful day. After they had eaten, they played about in the water a little, Alec teased and splashed and finally chased Parma on to the bank, and when he caught her, kissed her a little too ardently so that she had to beg him to desist. After that, she found it hard to relax with him, and he became silent, almost moody. She wondered if he were regretting now that he had forgone the company of the others. He lay face down on the grass, not talking, and soon from his even breathing she knew he had fallen asleep.

Parma got up and wandered away quietly in among the trees until the river and Alec were hidden from her and she was quite alone. There in the silence of the jungle she stood pensive, meditating, suddenly lonely and lost. She and Alec had had such fun in Sydney. They had seemed so close. Why was it so different here? She wasn't like that girl of Pierce's— she didn't need people, entertainments, artificial stimulants. And Alec—surely *he* didn't need them . . .

A blue butterfly, a black teardrop like a perfect distilled flourish at the tip of each shining azure wing, was hovering around her, and she watched it mindlessly, enjoying its movements, its colour. She reached out a hand—almost brushed it—and then it fluttered higher, and drifted away on a breath of wind. Parma, with eyes for nothing else, followed it until she lost it amidst the pink flowers of a huge rhododendron.

With a sigh, she turned back for the river.

Alec had just wakened and was looking for her. 'Where on earth did you get to?' He stretched out his hand. 'Come down here on the grass with me.'

Parma, remembering his ardent kisses, hung back.

'Let's take a walk, and do some talking,' she said, standing looking down at him, slender and childlike in her cotton dress with its small leafy design.

'We can talk while we lie on the grass. We'll talk about us.' His eyes were bright, his hair tousled, and the brown of his chest showed where his shirt was unbuttoned. Suddenly Parma shivered a little. Everything seemed so much more—basic here. So much closer to nature. She had never been the least bit afraid of Alec in the city—of his emotions, his passions.

'Don't you want to talk about us?'

What did he mean? Did he mean—their love for each other? And if he did, was she ready to talk about that yet? Parma knew she wasn't. There were so many things they still had to learn about each other. She sat down just beyond his reach.

'Tell me about your work, Alec.'

He groaned. 'Darling, you can't mean that! I don't want to talk about my work—that's not why I asked you to come up here.'

'Then shall I tell you what I've been doing the last few days?'

'Must you?'

'Don't you want to know?'

'Of course I want to know.' He sounded impatient. 'But just now I want to kiss you. Come here!' He moved towards her quickly and put his arm around her. Suddenly, in a panic, she wondered if she could handle him, here with the wild jungle all around and not another soul for miles. Her fear showed up plainly in the darkening of her eyes, and Alec grimaced and let her go.

'All right, then, tell me what you've been doing, for heaven's sake.'

He couldn't have said it more ungraciously, and she coloured deeply and launched confusedly into an over-bright recital about Helen's folk tales.

'I've been listening to some of the tapes,' she concluded. 'They're all in pidgin at present, and she's going to call her book *Tok Kuskus*. Do you understand pidgin, Alec?'

'Well, of course I do. How do you think I'd go about teaching the natives how to grow their crops otherwise?'

'I thought you might talk to them in their own language.'

'Good God! There are about seven hundred tribal languages in the Territory. That's rather the point of pidgin. It serves as an intertribal language.'

'Isn't it just—a funny sort of English?'

'No, it's not a funny sort of English. It has its own grammatical rules and is based more on the Melanesian languages than English.'

'I wish I could speak it, Alec. I only know a few things like *kaikai* and *maski*.'

'It wouldn't be any use to you. I know people who've been here for years and about all they can say is *Gutpela kai*, or *Raus*. You'd have no use for it, Parma.'

'But if I lived here,' Parma thought. Didn't Alec think of it that way? He was rolling himself a cigarette and she watched his brown fingers arranging the tobacco on the little square of paper, and she knew with a sinking heart that she was boring him. She said desperately, 'Alec, tell me about the Gides.'

He looked up sharply.

'What do you want to know about them? What have you heard?'

'Nothing much. But David and Pierce were talking about their plantation falling to rack and ruin and I got the idea you were going to help, but it all fell through.'

'So it did, but what of it? The Gides don't want to be helped. Anyone will tell you that. Though I can't see any of it's of interest to you.'

'No,' said Parma lamely. 'Alec, why did you ask me to come to New Guinea?'

He stared at her, raising his dark brows, and answered her over the flame of the match as he lit his cigarette. 'Why do you think, you little nitwit? Because I couldn't get you out of my mind. And now you won't even let me kiss you. Can you wonder I'm as cranky as a bear with a sore head?'

His eyes smiled at her, and there was all his charm again, and she felt herself weakening, softening. She moved impulsively into his arms. 'Oh, Alec, I'm sorry. It's the jungle.'

'Is that what it is? Well, next weekend I'll take you in to Kundalufa. We'll go to the native market in the morning and top off the day at the Sports Club. How will that be?'

'Fine,' she said, grateful for his forgiveness. The ground seemed firmer beneath her feet and she felt a bad passage was behind her.

The next day he made no attempt to get her to himself, but took her to visit friends, the Lowes, on a tea plantation. She loved the drive there, and the Highland scenery. There was beauty at every turn of the road, and his friends made her feel comfortable and at home. It didn't seem to matter that they treated her quite simply as a visitor to the Territory.

'You must take Parma to one of the little mountain towns,' they said. 'You must take her through the Cassam Pass to the Markham Valley.' They were full of suggestions.

'But don't for heaven's sake let him take you mountain climbing,' advised Marcia Lowe laughingly. 'It's true you'll get magnificent views, but the downward trip is not always worth it from the girl's point of view. It's generally been raining and it can be hell.' She grinned at Alec. 'Remember when you took Pauline up Mount Michael, Alec? Or was it that other girl, Danielle? It was the red-headed one at any rate, and she was absolutely livid—her lovely clothes ruined by all that mud.' She laughed across the tea trolley at Parma. 'I think the poor girl slid all the way down on her bottom, using her hands as brakes!'

So Alec had had other girls—lots of them, by all accounts. Well, Parma didn't mind that. After all, he was thirty-three, so it was to be expected. She had had other boy-friends—William Cunningham, to be exact, so she was not really very experienced, but at least she had learned that long friendships don't necessarily turn into true love. She couldn't really have loved William, whom she had known for years and years, or she would never have fallen in love with Alec so soon afterwards.

At any rate, she enjoyed Sunday thoroughly and was ready to put Saturday's confusion down as a day of necessary readjustment.

She had scarcely seen Helen all weekend, and on Monday the two of them settled down to spend an hour or two on *Tok Kuskus*. Helen played through a couple of stories about, respectively, a spirit woman and a devil-pig. Parma listened carefully to the pidgin English, but could not make much of it, and Helen switched the tape off every few seconds to translate. As the stories began to take form it occurred to Parma that she might be able to do little drawings to illustrate them. It would probably please no one but herself, but it would be something pleasant to do when Alec was not there. When the tape was finally switched off, they talked a little about the weekend. Parma was curious about the Gides. Alec had not wanted to talk about them and she was fairly certain that the reason he had opted out of joining the swimming picnic was because he preferred not to meet them.

'I was sorry we didn't come to the picnic,' she told Helen. 'I don't think Alec wanted to see the Gides.'

'Possibly not,' Helen agreed non-committally. 'They can be hard to get on with. One makes the effort to be friendly because they're so young and because they've had so much misfortune.'

'Have they been married long?'

Helen gave her a quick look. 'Arthur and Sophie are brother and sister. Sophie's nineteen and Arthur must be about twenty-three—too young and inexperienced to take on the task of getting a dying concern back on its feet.'

'Then why is he trying to do it? You were all talking about it the other night and I felt curious.'

'It's quite a story—and a sad one,' said Helen, looking out into the garden where birds and butterflies darted and hovered in a riot of bright flowers. 'It all hinges on the fact that Ngaire Gide should never have married a planter. She left her husband—Richard—as soon as Arthur and Sophie were sent away to school, and he simply couldn't cope with life on his own. He started drinking—we all knew it, but none of us could do a thing about it. He didn't care what happened to the plantation, he lost all concern for his labourers, for his trees. Then one night driving back from a wild weekend in Kundalufa he knocked a native boy down, and the tribe descended on his bungalow with bows and arrows and spears.'

Parma's eyes widened. 'That sort of thing can happen?'

'Yes. Tribal vengeance is an elementary form of justice. Many of the natives understand nothing else. Richard would most likely have been killed if Pierce hadn't happened to come along at the strategic moment.'

'What did Pierce do?' Parma was shivering a little.

Helen shrugged. 'He never talks about it. But he has a lot of influence with the natives—they respect him, he's the great white *Masta*. At any rate, though Richard escaped with his life, by the time Arthur was through his Ag. Science course, Kunai Valley was in a hopeless mess. To cap it all, Richard had a stroke and died only a couple of months later, leaving Sophie and

61

Arthur on their own. Unfortunately, Arthur is so touchy and proud, so stupidly sure he can set everything right on his own, that no one seems able to help him.'

'David implied the other night that Alec was going to do something.'

'That may be so.' Helen made a sketchy gesture with her hand. It seemed to imply, 'If you want to know about that you'll have to ask Alec'. But Parma had asked, and had learned exactly nothing.

Helen began gathering up her papers. 'I'm going to take a swim. Are you coming?'

The conversation was obviously at an end. Parma said 'Yes.' The thought of the pool was attractive, and she would be very sure to come home when Helen did. She was not going to be caught there alone by Pierce Adams again.

A day or so later, however, she had an unexpected encounter with him in the garden. She was sitting in the shade of a hibiscus that flaunted huge yellow flowers, sketching. Helen was at work on her *Tok Kuskus*, but there was nothing ready for her to type. She had been thinking of Alec, wondering if he would manage to come out to the plantation one night before the weekend. The weekends seemed so very far apart. They would never get to know each other thoroughly this way, and she felt that their relationship was almost at a standstill. She couldn't imagine what she would have done if she hadn't been lucky enough to encounter Helen Barlow. She would probably have had to go back to Australia *kwiktaim*, and as it was, she could hardly expect to stay on with the Barlows indefinitely. It was a very tricky situation.

The story of Ngaire Gide had made her superconscious of how important it was for a man in the Territory to choose the right wife, and though Parma had a good imagination she somehow could not picture the life of a Didirman's wife. She wished rather

62

desperately that she could have gone to Varmari. If only that anthropologist hadn't been occupying the guest house, she would have insisted on staying there herself. Here, she was a princess locked in a tower . . .

She was completely immersed in her thoughts and the sketch grew mindlessly from her fingers. She had brought some squeakers with her and her drawing was a coloured one—large, simple, clear. She looked up and saw Pawpaw, Unkapenna's wife, graceful and pretty in a red and white shift, a yellow hibiscus in her short frizzy hair, go by with the tiny brown child Elisabet, who wore her usual beaded waistband and grass skirt.

Parma made to turn the page, and at that moment Pierce Adams' taunting voice exclaimed, 'It's Penelope and her tapestry, I do believe!'

He stood before her, aggressively male in his light shirt open almost to the waist, and white shorts against which his muscular legs looked like mahogany. One brown hand rested against the trunk of the hibiscus tree, and a butterfly flitted over the dark gold of his hair, fragile and inconsequential against his positive masculinity.

Parma looked up at him mutely and felt the familiar shiver of apprehension that his presence seemed to induce. His eyes, green-gold this afternoon, watched her languorously.

'I suppose you know the story of Penelope, Miss Drew?'

She nodded, her eyes wide, wary. She wondered what he was going to say, sure it would be something aimed to discomfit her.

'Of course you do. That little head of yours will have been well stuffed with all the pleasant old legends . . . Penelope, while her husband was absent, kept her many suitors at bay by busily working on a tapestry that was somehow never finished.' He heaved his long length away from the tree and two strides brought him close to her. 'Are you using your sketch pad as a wall of safety, Miss Drew? Do you equate your Didirman with Odysseus? Does the weekend and when you will see him again seem a lifetime away?'

Parma, with a quick movement, had turned her sketch pad on its face. She didn't know why, but she didn't want him to see her drawing. It was as if it were secret, instead of being a simple childish thing of no importance. His eyebrows went up ironically and he screwed up one eye and considered her, and she knew in her heart that she was not going to escape his gibes, that this was only a temporary relief.

'Of course I knew I would find you at this sort of thing. I knew you wouldn't have the courage to go out and discover the real face of the Territory. Your little adventure at the river the other day scared you properly, didn't it?' His eyes were cruelly mocking and she felt her face flame. She knew that he had meant to frighten her—that his savage embrace, his unwanted kiss, had been meant as a symbol of the dangers she could expect to find in this primitive land. And she knew now that he expected her to take care she didn't expose herself to any further upsetting experiences.

'Well, let's see your tapestry, Penelope. What is it? *Samting nating*? Or *samting tiru*?'

There was no future in putting up any opposition. She handed him the sketch pad passively, resignedly, and waited for his derision. She had drawn a little girl with floating dark hair and hands outstretched towards a blue and black butterfly that flew just beyond her reach.

'Hmm, very pretty,' he said after a few seconds' contemplation of the drawing. 'You've got our Blue Mountain butterfly there—and not too badly observed either, for a newcomer. What's it supposed to signify, by the way?'

Until that exact moment, Parma hadn't really known that it signified anything. She had drawn

64

mindlessly, freely. Now she was acutely aware of what she had been expressing. The dark-haired child reaching out so eagerly was, of course, herself. And the butterfly—equally *of course*—was the butterfly of love...

She said quickly, defensively, 'Nothing. It doesn't signify anything at all. It's just—it's—*samting nating.*'

He seemed amused at her use of the pidgin phrase. All the same—'The psychologists would tell you differently,' he said dryly. '*Samting tiru!* May I have it?'

The pad was back in her hands. She looked at her picture and knew that it would give her no more joy. The Adams man was making fun of her—and it. She was sure, too, that he knew what it meant. The symbolism was so totally elementary. And he would think her search for love foolish, stupidly romantic and unrealistic. Parma Drew searching for love here—in *his* land.

She said briefly, 'Yes, you can have it,' and tore it from the pad with such deliberate carelessness that it was ripped in two. She looked up at him with a gleam of triumph in her eyes.

He took the two pieces and drawled out, 'What a pity you did that! Elisabet would have loved it.'

So he had wanted it for Elisabet! Well, what had she imagined? Had she imagined he would pin it up on his wall as an amusing reminder of a foolish romantic girl who had come to a tough country imagining that love was a pretty butterfly?

She said, 'I'll mend it—I'll give it to Elisabet.'

'*I'll* mend it,' said Pierce.

She knew he would not. She knew that he simply liked to be the *Masta.* She stood up.

'Please yourself,' she said indifferently. 'I'm going back to the bungalow.'

He did not follow her.

For some reason she could not get his taunting out of her mind. 'I knew you wouldn't have the courage to go out and discover the real face of the Territory.' Parma thought of Ngaire Gide who had destroyed a man's life because she had not learned to love and live with his land. She thought of Rowena Arnold who had promised Pierce Adams she would marry him and then had opted out, because she could not forgo the easy lure of civilisation. Parma knew that she must find out for herself whether this land, this life, could bring her fulfilment, provided they came hand in hand with love. She had no wish to ruin either her own or anyone else's life by making a wrong choice...

Her chance to take action of a sort came one day when Helen was busy with some dressmaking.

'It's a peach of a day,' Helen said. 'I'd go out and enjoy it if David and I didn't have this dinner engagement on Thursday. I simply must have something new to wear! You've been sitting over the typewriter all morning, Parma—why don't you take my car and go out? You're perfectly welcome, you know.' She had offered her car to Parma before, but the girl had always been too diffident to accept it. Now she felt differently, for it was one way of taking up Pierce's challenge. All the same, she hesitated an instant.

'It doesn't do to be too timid in the Territory,' Helen coaxed. 'Come on now, there's no need to be afraid of the natives, and so long as you stick to the beaten track you can't come to much harm. I'll draw you a little map if you like so you can visit some of the beauty spots. It'll all be very safe, I promise you.'

'*Maski*,' said Parma lightly. 'I don't want a map.' She saw Helen blink, and she felt thoughtful. Did Helen too see her as completely unadventurous? Was she, in her gentle way, trying to push and prod Parma into a realisation that she must think hard before she fooled herself she wanted to stay here—before she allowed herself to fall in love with Alec beyond the point of recall? 'If I'm to do any exploring, then I may as well do the thing properly, mightn't I, and work it all out for myself! I'm not *really* a stay-at-home, you know.' Her eyes sparkled a little. 'I somehow think you all have the impression that I have a loving family waiting back home to gather me safely back into the nest. But I've been alone in the world for a long time. It's years and years since anyone's worried about me. I came all the way out to Australia on my own, so it's hardly going to bother me to drive a few miles up into the mountains.'

'Brave words,' said Helen dryly. 'But you're right back at the starting line when you come to the Territory.' Her smile tempered her words. 'Anyhow, if that's the way you feel, fine! Off you go! Just see you're home before dark, that's all.'

Twenty minutes later Parma was on her way, driving down the long road between the coffee trees, then, once clear of the plantation, heading away from Kundalufa. Pierce, she knew, had gone to the Gides' plantation some time during the morning. From the safety of the verandah room where she was typing, she had heard him call out to Helen. She didn't know where the Kunai Valley Estate was, but she reckoned on being safe from Pierce, at any rate.

At first she drove sedately, a little nervous of the car. She had got her driver's licence in England—William had taught her to drive—and lately she had driven Miss Webster's car on a few occasions when the headmistress had wanted some errand done. As she left the plantation behind, she gained in confidence and began to drive steadily and to grow accustomed to the roughness of the road, so that she was able to look around her a little.

She drove past native villages, with their clusters of round thatched primitive-looking huts; past subsistence gardens that made patches of green against the hillsides. She saw the native women, backs bent, dig-

67

ging and weeding; she saw men clearing trees to make new gardens; a few brown children waved to her. She drove through heavy jungle, then past great smooth slopes of waving kunai grass. There was more jungle and the road wound on and on, gently up and up, towards distant mountains that disappeared into the clouds. Parma knew she would never reach those mountains and slowly a feeling of defeat began to overtake her. It was all so quiet and peaceful! Except for the beautiful scenery and the native villages she might as well have been driving around the Australian countryside. Challenge there was none. She could imagine Pierce Adams' mockery! Soon she would turn the car around and drive meekly home again. And what would she have accomplished? Exactly nothing...

It was at that moment that she saw a turn-off a little way ahead. It was quite definitely off the beaten track, and while the road she was following led up into the ranges, this track went down through thick jungle into some hidden valley.

It took Parma only an instant to make up her mind. She swung right and began to follow the bumpy little track, her heart in her mouth because it was so narrow that every now and then the car brushed against bamboo or kunai grass, that made a soft, hissing, rush-rush sound.

Then, taking a sharp hairpin bend, she found herself suddenly and terrifyingly confronted by a great swaying truck driven by a native in a khaki shirt. She could see his white teeth as he grinned at her, could hear the grinding and roaring as the huge dust-covered truck came towards her ... She pulled madly, desperately, on the wheel, felt perspiration break out on her forehead. And Helen's car was sinking into soft dirt and a wall of kunai canes.

The truck with its load of coffee beans grazed past and went merrily on its way, round the bend and out of sight in three seconds. But Parma, in Helen's car, was well and truly stuck. The engine had stalled, and no amount of starting and revving would get it moving. She climbed out of the car and had a look. The wheels were deep in mud and soft earth. Parma looked around her. Beyond the kunai grass, thick jungle. Not a village or a garden to be seen. Down the road ahead, more jungle. Parakeets screeched and the red and flame of tropical flowers glowed. Far off, the magical enchanted sound of a gong vibrated on the air—*belo* from some distant plantation.

Parma had no idea what to do. Whether to leave the car and start walking in the hope of reaching the plantation—which sounded as if it were miles and miles away—or whether to have just one more try to get the car moving first, although she knew in advance that it was hopeless. Finally, she got in behind the wheel once more and set the motor turning over.

When she looked up, her heart leapt into her mouth. Coming at a run from the jungle ahead was a crowd of natives, their faces and bodies painted with clay, their heads decked with fantastic headdresses of tall swaying feathers that shimmered and glinted in the sun. They looked utterly wild and primitive—straight out of the Stone Age—and they carried black bows and arrows like the ones she had seen in the planter's bungalow. The story Helen had told of vengeful natives attacking Richard Gide sprang frighteningly into her mind.

And all the while this wildly dancing horde was coming closer and closer—and they were making straight for the car!

CHAPTER FIVE

THERE was nothing to do but stay where she was. But, had her life depended on it, Parma could not have moved. And perhaps it did, was the wild thought that flashed through her mind. One particularly bizarre native was ahead of the others, and Parma, half mesmerised, watched him come nearer. His face was painted with red clay and there were rings of yellow around his eyes and a slender curved bone through his nose.

He stopped a yard or so from the car and his followers stopped their mad race too, and stood staring, some way back. Parma's heart began to beat so hard and so loudly that she thought they must all hear it, when the leader spoke.

'*Motoka bilong Missis i dai, laka?*' The soft sound of the pidgin words was oddly reassuring, and at once Parma could feel some of her tension ebbing. '*Mipela laik siubim nau. Yu savvy?*'

Parma didn't altogether *savvy*. She shook her head, sought for words—words she had heard Helen use to Witni, words from the tapes, words Alec had used— any words at all that might help. She came out with, '*Nogat. Mi no tok pisin.*' And she bit her lip, her eyes wide. What happened now?

What happened was that the spokesman turned and called out to his tribe in their own language, and a minute later a dozen or so of them had surrounded the car, and, crushing back the long kunai grass, were lifting it bodily back on to the road. Parma could feel herself trembling, though she was sure they only meant to help her now. Then, as they pressed around the car, their faces at the windows, close, so close, she felt fear rise in her once more. Those strange unreal

70

faces covered in red and yellow clay, those shaking plumes, and swaying strings of shells—those strange shining black eyes—— What if they wouldn't let her go on? She wished she could speak pidgin, heard her shaken voice saying over and over, 'Thank you—thank you very much——' And all they did was to stare and stare.

Then suddenly they began to fall back. An authoritative voice was exclaiming, '*Orait. Yupela lukim tumas Misis. Em i pesin nogut.*'

Pierce Adams' tall form swam into Parma's vision, his eyes sharp and alive with a mixture of exasperation and concern. 'Are you all right, Miss Drew?'

'Yes, of course,' she said with dignity, though her voice shook and she knew her face was drained of colour. 'I—I've been trying to tell them how—how grateful I am——'

The shadow of a smile passed across his face, but he nodded, turned away, and said a few quick words. Parma made an effort to calm down. She looked out at the natives as if to reassure herself that she hadn't been carried away by one of her flights of fancy. It was hard to tell in these fantastic, sensational Highlands if one was simply seeing visions or if it was all there. But Pierce was real enough, towering above the weird bunch of natives with their Paradise plumes and cuscus fur and strings of shells, and talking to them as easily as if they had met in a city street.

'They're on their way to a *singsing*, Miss Drew. Hence the regalia.'

'A—a *singsing*?' repeated Parma, her voice still maddeningly uncertain.

'Yes. They tell me they're giving a feast in return for past hospitality from another village. *Oli wokim singsing longen nau.*' He smiled slightly and Parma, when some of the natives looked her way, managed a smile too.

A minute later they were running and dancing

down through the jungle, and Pierce, with a brisk movement, gave all his attention to Parma.

'Move over, Miss Drew, and let's see if the car's in working order.'

'It is,' said Parma, not budging. 'It was just stuck in the mud.'

He took no notice of her implied refusal of his request, but opened the door and, short of putting up a fight, there was nothing for her to do but to move over. He climbed into the seat as she slid along and his presence seemed to fill the car. He turned the ignition key, set the motor going.

'Hmm, seems to be all right. You shouldn't be on this road, you know. For one thing, it's strictly for four-wheel drives. For another, you don't know where you're heading. Do you?' He switched off the engine as he spoke and swung round abruptly to face her so that she found herself confronted by those oddly coloured eyes that were regarding her relentlessly.

She didn't answer his question. She knew that he was right. She had disobeyed Helen's instructions and taken a chance. And she had been punished for it.

'You're thinking you got off lightly—that Fate was on your side. Well, you can forget about that. I saw you coming down the hill, Miss Drew. I saw that truck hogging the road. It's a habit with truck drivers here, be they white or brown or whatever, to think they own the roads. And it's a fact *you* had no right on it. I could have come up and pulled you out—my jeep's along the road a piece and I always carry a tow-rope—but——' He shrugged and grinned a little and Parma drew in her breath. He had seen those natives—perhaps he had even sent them. He had wanted her to be frightened, he had wanted to demonstrate forcibly the sort of thing she was likely to encounter in this barbarous jungle. Did he hope he was going to frighten her out of his country? Which was not, she corrected herself, *his* country any more than it was—well, the

Barlows'—and *they* were quite happy to have her there. As a guest, her mind added automatically.

So Parma shrugged too. 'I'm glad you didn't. It was much more exciting the way it was. Those stunning get-ups! I thought I must be dreaming!'

That made him look at her again and she saw the corner of his mouth twitch.

A brown finger touched her cheek and she flinched. 'Dreaming? Or having a nightmare? You were frightened, Miss Drew. You've lost all your pretty colour and I can practically hear your heart beating.' His hand dropped from her face and his fingers took hold of her wrist. 'Like me to take your pulse?'

She pulled away from him as if his touch had burned her. Her tongue touched her upper lip and he said tauntingly, 'Did you wonder if the natives were going to kill and eat you?'

She closed her eyes and tried to move away from him. He was intolerable—and he was doing his best to ridicule her. She said with an effort, 'Of course I didn't. I'm not as ignorant of your country as you suppose.'

'No? You're still *tumas* ignorant, you know. You've a heap to learn. And I doubt whether there's any point in your learning it.'

'You still class me as an outsider, don't you? You think I can't adjust, and you're determined for some reason that I shan't. Well, let me tell you this——' as she spoke she felt the colour coming back into her face with a vengeance. 'If a woman loves a man—really loves him—she will go with him anywhere—anywhere!'

She saw his eyes harden and a nerve jump at the corner of his mouth and she knew she had flicked him where it hurt. He was not the only one who could be cruel! She knew too that she had pretty well implied love for Alec and her own implication unsettled her. She was not by any means sure whether she would say

Yes to Alec if he should ask her to share his life. But if she did say No it would not be because she found life in the Territory unacceptable. It was an exciting and awesome country, and for her it had a very strong appeal.

She glanced away from the planter into the dark shadows of the jungle where sunlight filtering made splashes and streaks of colour, and when her gaze came back to him, there was a new expression on his face. It was watchful, wary, almost listening—as if he too were asking himself a question. She wondered what that question was.

She drew an uneven breath.

'May I be on my way now?'

'Where *is* your way?'

'I've come this far—I may as well go on.'

He appeared to consider that and she felt infuriated. What she did was no concern of his. He said finally, 'All right. We'll follow the *singsing*, shall we? We haven't been invited to attend, but we can have a look at least. Seeing,' he finished, starting up the car once again, 'seeing that you're so eager to pack a bit of out-of-the-way sightseeing into your visit.' His voice was soft, almost kind, and she looked at him distrustfully. But she was not at all averse to taking a look at that *singsing*, and it was indisputable that a guide, an escort, would be an asset.

She'd have gone on in any case, supposing he had not turned up. Or she *thought* she would have gone on—once her nerves had stopped jumping and her hands had stopped shaking and her heart had stopped pounding. The fact that she was now completely steady could not be due entirely to the fact that she had to put on a good show for Pierce Adams.

She said nonchalantly, 'That suits me very well, Mr Adams.'

He gave her an oblique look. 'Suppose we tone

down the formality. Try calling me Pierce, will you—Parma.'

'I'll try,' she agreed. Then as he drove the car expertly down the narrow twisting road, she asked, 'Do *you* know where we're heading, Mr—Pierce?'

'Yes. There's a *singsing* ground in the valley.' He found a place to park the car further down, and then they began to climb up through thick jungle to a place where they could look down on the ceremonial ground. Parma was wearing flimsy sandals not meant for walking and she found the going slippery. Several times Pierce had to stop and wait for her, or to offer his hand to help her up a particularly steep pinch. She was perspiring and breathing with difficulty when they finally emerged at the top of a slope and stopped.

Looking down over dense matted jungle, Parma could see the *singsing* ground, and she stood breathing shallowly, trying to catch her breath and unable yet to speak. There was a long cleared patch of ground away below, sheltered all round by a protective belt of bamboo. At one end of the long ceremonial ground was a rectangular space upon which was converging a troop of plumed dancers led by drummers. Even away up here, the rhythmic beat of the throbbing kundu drums could be heard and Parma could see clearly through air which had a sharp crystal quality that these drums were shaped like an hourglass and had a skin stretched tightly over one end. Beyond the rectangular clearing was a stretch of brown earth and down its length at either side were long shed-like buildings with thatched roofs and open sides. A great table was covered with rows and rows of overlapping banana leaves, and on them were laid out piles of food. Women and children, their brown near-naked bodies gleaming with pig fat, crowded down towards the dancers, while from the jungle at either side came a continual stream of more dancers, more spectators.

Parma took in the scene as one in a trance, and at

last her breathing became easier. The beat of the kundu drums, throbbing, persistent, was like the steady beating of a heart, the heart of this strange almost undiscovered country ...

She became aware that the tall man lounging against a tree just a little behind her had diverted his attention to her.

'Recovered your breath?' he asked dryly. 'You look a frail girl, and you *are* a frail girl. Our mountains are too tough for you, *laka*?'

She said, 'I'll admit I'm not in training for strenuous walking. But your legs are longer than mine and you set a torrid pace, Mr Adams.'

'Pierce,' he corrected her laconically. His hand came out to rest lightly on her shoulder. 'I'm sorry if I rushed you. I'm not used to escorting small girls through the jungle.'

'I'll forgive you the rush,' said Parma lightly, too much aware of his touch. 'It was worth it to see the *singsing*. What happens next?'

'There'll be various displays of dancing. Then later they'll light a fire and cook the food and the feast will be on. Some of them—the visitors—will sleep in the rest houses that have been built for that purpose. And then tomorrow, the whole thing will start up again.'

'For how long?'

'Until the food runs out.' He sent her a smile that was pure amusement.

They watched for some time longer. The dancing continued with much stamping of feet, and the beat of the kundu drums, the weird sound of the singing rose upwards from what was now a sparkling kaleidoscope of colour. Soon clouds began to swarm across the sky and a chill air to descend and Parma shivered a little. Down below, men were dragging wood into a pile and then the bright red and yellow of flame leapt up, and a plume of smoke rose and spread so that the scene in the valley seemed faded and unreal, as if it would float or blow away.

'Time we were moving. You're cold.' Pierce Adams' voice roused the girl as from a dream. He held out his hand to her and unthinkingly she took it. It was hard and warm and strong and as he led her down the steep hillside through the heavy undergrowth she hung on to it as if it were something quite impersonal—as perhaps it was.

They went fast and her leg muscles were beginning to ache, but she didn't complain. She would be stiff tomorrow, that was for sure. When they reached the road he said, 'It'll be dark in no time,' and suddenly she seemed to come to her senses and to realise how tightly she was holding on to his hand. But when she attempted to release herself, she found his fingers strongly intertwined with hers and bit her lip in sudden fear that he was going to repeat his performance of that evening at the pool, when he had embraced her so savagely and meaninglessly.

Instead, he let her go as soon as they reached the car.

'I'll have to pick up the jeep,' he said abruptly. 'I'll need it tomorrow. You'll have to follow me up that track and keep close. It's unlikely we'll meet another truck, but if we do, then get over into the muck—don't imagine for an instant the truck driver will give you room. If you get stuck I'll pull you out.'

As it happened he didn't have to come to her rescue, for which she was thankful. But her nerves were still tense when they finally emerged on to the main road and turned towards the plantation. Parma knew she was going to be glad to get home—to take a hot relaxing bath, and to change out of these sandals. She had seen some of the real territory—it was not much, but it was a little—and the encounter had left her slightly bruised.

It was dark when they reached the Butterfly Montane Estate, and Pierce Adams took it upon himself to deliver her to Helen, but he told no tales.

'We met up and I took this girl for a bird's eye view of a village *singsing*. I hope you didn't worry, Helen.'

'Just a little,' Helen admitted. 'Will you stay for dinner, Pierce? It's just about ready.'

'No, thanks. Unkapenna will have some *kai* ready for me. By the way, you might tell David I got hold of a few husky fellows from one of the villages who're going to present themselves at Gides when the *singsing*'s over. I'll have to check up tactfully, but I'm hoping for the best.' He raised a hand in a sketchy goodbye and followed Parma, who was going to change her shoes, through the door. She heard his voice, low and close, as he murmured, 'I suppose you'll be back to drawing butterflies tomorrow. Or will your next picture have a rather more fearsome content?'

Parma gave a slight shrug. 'I shouldn't imagine so.' She sent him the ghost of a smile over her shoulder, and stifled a yawn. She felt unutterably exhausted, but she was not ready to show a white flag.

Despite her bravado, she dreamed of that encounter on the mountain road—of the grotesque and frightening faces that had pressed around the car, seeming to menace her. It had been a very bad moment, but she would never suffer in that particular way again. Waking in fright from her nightmare, hearing her own heartbeats like the beat of distant kundu drums, she assured herself of this.

She confessed to Helen the following day that she had left the beaten track and got into a spot of bother, but Helen only laughed. 'Oh, everyone does it at some time or another—it's the lure of the forbidden. It was lucky for you that Pierce was out Kunai Valley way. Did you meet any of the villagers?'

'Not—socially,' Parma said, and then laughed aloud. 'I mean, I wasn't with Pierce while he was recruiting labour, if that's what you mean.'

'We have yet to see how that turns out,' mused Helen. 'It's pretty sure the natives will turn up for a day or two out of respect for Pierce. But after that, it's anybody's guess what will happen and depends on Arthur's somewhat doubtful abilities in the field of applied psychology. His father's reputation hangs on with the villagers, I'm afraid, and I personally find Arthur a rather unprepossessing young man. He's sulky and belligerent and very hard to get through to.'

'And—Sophie?' Parma didn't know why she asked it.

'Oh, Sophie is just a silly child.' Helen changed the subject. 'I'm going over to the natives' quarters today. One of the children has some troublesome leg sores and I told David I'd attend to them. Would you like to come?'

'Yes, please.'

Helen got her first-aid box and they walked together through the garden and past the shaded coffee groves where natives in laplaps or shorts were hard at work weeding and pruning. The families who lived on the estate had simple timber cottages, and gardens where they grew their own *kaukau* and a variety of other vegetables—tomatoes, cucumbers, pumpkin, sweet corn. Women in cotton dresses were tending the gardens just as if they had been in their own villages. Some of them carried babies in *bilums*, and some had little girl children at their sides who were digging in the ground with small pointed sticks.

'Not many of those little girls will grow up to become gardeners,' Helen commented as they drew near. 'They'll go off to mission or government schools and some of them will be nurses and some will be teachers or weavers or typists. It's a rapidly changing world in the Highlands, and that thin skin of civilisation is growing thicker all the time so that one day it will be a protective covering ... Torea!' she called, seeing the woman she wanted. '*Mi laik lukim sikpela leg bilong picanini meri.*'

Torea was pretty with large dark eyes and a lovely smile. Her frizzy hair was cut short and her skin shone, but her little girl, Rebeka, just now looked a very dirty little girl, and her legs looked very sore.

'*Tumas giraun nogut,*' Helen said sternly. '*Moa waswas,* Torea.' She held out her arms to the child who ran to her mother and clung to her legs, peeping out at Parma. '*Yu bringim picanini nisaet haus nau,* Torea.'

Parma didn't go into the house. They were shy of her, and Helen would cope better on her own. But in no time at all she was surrounded by a bevy of small children who appeared from nowhere, unabashed in their tiny grass skirts, staring, giggling, one or two of the bolder ones coming to touch her—her bare white legs and arms.

'*Wonem naem bilong yu?*' she asked, but they giggled and ran away. Parma wished she had her sketch pad and squeakers so that she could amuse them.

The next morning when she went with Helen she took her largest drawing pad and a handful of brightly coloured squeakers, and when Helen disappeared with Torea and Rebeka, she sat down on the ground and began to draw. She drew a child—a little brown child, this time. She drew a flower—a big red hibiscus. She made a green square of garden and drew a fence around it with bold strong strokes. She drew a *meri* with a *bilum* over her shoulder and a baby's head appearing from it.

By now there was a crowd of children around her. They had forgotten their shyness and their giggles and were watching absorbedly. Parma began to draw a butterfly, and one of them touched the blue wing shape and said, '*Bimbi!*' in a tone of great satisfaction, and Parma, without knowing why, looked up and saw Pierce Adams there, watching her with mocking amusement.

She flushed crimson and the children all stared at Pierce who said, tilting his eyebrows, '*Bimbi?* Don't tell me you're at it again, Parma Drew. I expected bows and arrows and the terror of the mountains this time. Unqualified surrender, complete adjustment.' Three strides and he was looking down at the drawing too. 'I'm afraid you're just a soft romantic girl,' he said, and she remembered—'Sugar and spice—you'll melt in the rain.' Her small pink tongue licked nervously at her upper lip. A little naked child touched her hand, touched the blue squeaker she was holding, and Parma drew a second butterfly. She was beginning to think that the butterfly was equivalent to her signature—the butterfly of love. Pierce strode off as though he could not be bothered with such a foolish creature, and she looked thoughtfully after his retreating back and then wrote in bold letters, 'Yours truly—a romantic dreamer'...

Helen had finished the dress she was making, Parma had turned up the hem for her. It was Thursday night, and Alec had not been in touch. The Barlows were going out to dinner and Parma was to prepare her own.

'Sorry about this,' apologised Helen. 'I wish we could take you along to the Garfields', but Ann works her dinners out with mathematical precision—guestwise, that is. There's always lashings of food. She's had this planned for a month. You'll be all right, won't you?'

'Perfectly,' said Parma. She was planning a drawing to illustrate a story about the devil-pig—a fabled beast of monstrous size and terrifying aspect—that was featured in a couple of the stories Helen had collected. She had a new conception of the feeling of fear and felt she could treat the subject adequately—could see in her mind's eye vague shadowy figures with head plumes and bows and arrows lurking in the background while the huge pig roamed the jungle, dwarfing the giant tree ferns. 'I shall probably give myself nightmare,' she reflected as Helen and David drove off at sunset into light that seemed to be filtered through red silk, and made the garden glow warm and unreal and dramatic.

She stayed on the verandah for a while listening to the sounds of evening—shouts and laughter echoing from the natives' quarters, uncertain notes played on a guitar by Rebeka's father, Kwalibu. A flock of chattering cockatoos flew down to some pool to drink and wind rustled faintly in the casuarina trees that sheltered the precious coffee bushes. Over it all hung the pervasive scent of the ginger blossom—so sweet and subtle and maddening that Parma thought she would never forget it. It was a scent that belonged to the darkness and the rain rather than to this strange red sunset glow. She glanced over towards the planter's bungalow, though she had promised herself she would not. She knew a pang that he was over there alone. Helen had said, 'You'll be safe enough. Pierce is there, he's doing some paper work.'

'And I am here alone,' thought Parma, turning away and walking slowly into the house. She went out to the kitchen and with an effort—though why it should need an effort she did not know—called Alec into her thoughts, Alec's face into her mind. She stood still contemplating her mental image—Alec without a beard, suave, smiling, dressed in a dark lounge suit and standing close at her side while they piled their plates with smorgasbord food. It was like a dream. It belonged with things that no longer had any existence.

Slowly, Parma moved, and opened the refrigerator. There was some cold chicken—a bowl of tomatoes. She would make herself a sandwich.

She had not quite begun when a voice called, 'Parma!' and she jumped, thinking it was Alec's voice.

She hurried into the hallway and a silhouette, black against the fading glow of the sky, stood outlined. She knew at once that it was not Alec and her heart did something. Did it sink or did it leap? If it leapt—it was for nostalgic musings interrupted.

'Yes?'

'Come over to the bungalow and share my *kaikai*. If not for my sake then for the *hausboi*'s. For some reason he's taken a fancy to you.'

'I was going to make a sandwich,' said Parma. The glow from the sky was reflected on her face and she hoped it hid the tide of colour that had risen to her cheeks.

'Then hold it. Witni passed on the news that you were on your own—and a feast has been prepared.' She could discern his features now, could see the smile hovering on his lips, ironical, fleeting. 'Roast stuffed chicken and bacon rolls.'

Parma remembered that Helen had told her that was another dish Rowena Arnold had taught Unkapenna to cook. 'Another memorial feast,' she thought wryly, and she didn't think she wanted to share it. He would be thinking of Rowena Arnold—he had some sort of a love–hate relationship with his memories, she thought. He would be moody, unfriendly, ready to point up all her faults and shortcomings, hating her because she reminded him of Rowena.

She hesitated and he taunted her, 'You're afraid to dine alone with me, are you? I assure you the *hausboi* will be hanging around making sure you appreciate his efforts. You can come home straight after coffee if that's the way you want it. I'm a bit insistent because Unkapenna has spent hours on this dinner with you in mind and I don't want him offended.'

'All right, then.' Her lips twisted. 'Thank you, I'll come.'

'I suppose you'd like to change?'

'Yes, please.'

'I'll give you half an hour.'

He strode off and she watched him thoughtfully before she went inside. She was remembering that strange questioning look on his face when she had told him that if a girl loved a man she would go with him anywhere; and she was remembering how he had said, 'You're just a soft romantic girl.'

She didn't know why she thought of those two things, nor why her thoughts should make her shiver suddenly...

She took a shower and changed into a sleeveless yellow and white cotton with a full, ankle-length, divided skirt. It was graceful and not quite formal, and she wore a gold belt with it. She looped her hair back and caught it with a narrow gold ribbon, made up her face with a light touch, and looking at herself in the long mirror had the excited feeling of a dinner date ahead of her. Was that the reaction of a city girl who thrived on sophistication?

A chiffon scarf around her shoulders, she stepped carefully out in her yellow sandals, through the scented garden—and found the planter waiting for her by the gate. Above, the sky had grown dark, a few stars shone, and clouds drifted soft as mist. She could feel dew on her cheeks.

'You look charming,' he said. But he said it formally. He gave her his arm and they proceeded towards his bungalow. Music difted across on the cool night air—kundu drums and the weird wild sound of the mambu flute. It was so much a part of the night and the country that she shivered with compulsive recognition and acceptance.

'Are you cold?'

'No. It's the music.'

'You don't like it?' There was a hint of amusement in his voice.

'Of course I do.' But she didn't try to explain the

attraction it had for her. She wondered who had chosen it—Pierce Adams or his *hausboi*. And she wondered too if Rowena Arnold had liked the sound of kundu drums and the strange mambu ...

CHAPTER SIX

DINNER at the long table with its red cloth was a dream, and Pierce Adams set himself out to be the perfect host.

He spoke of the music, whose steady beat was putting Parma into something of a trance, lulling her into a feeling of harmony with the night and with her surroundings. He had recorded this music on tape himself, he told her, and he described the instruments—the carved bamboo that was made into a flute, the kundu drum that was shaped like an hourglass, and had a skin—animal or iguana—stretched over one end, and was beaten with the hand.

The *hausboi* moved quietly around the table or stood by the door watching Parma for signs of appreciation. Before she and the planter went into the sitting room for coffee, he brought her a gift—a little basket made from a palm leaf, the fronds cunningly interwoven, the stem curved back to make a handle. It was filled with fresh red strawberries, cushioned on a thick bed of leaves.

Parma's eyes shone. 'It's beautiful! Thank you, Unkapenna. Did Pawpaw make the basket?'

He told her, '*Yesa!*' and then with a little shake of his head exclaimed, 'Ah—*Wantok bilong mi, ia!*' and grinned at Pierce.

Pierce, his expression sardonic, translated. 'He says you're his kind of person.' His hand rested lightly on her shoulder as they went through the slatted doors. 'Come along and we'll have our coffee.'

Parma felt flattered—by Unkapenna, not by Pierce, who she was sure didn't share the *hausboi*'s good opinion of her.

She put her basket of strawberries carefully on a low

table and while she drank her coffee her eyes continually strayed to it. The native music had come to an end, and Pierce asked her what she would like to hear next.

'Could we please have the kundu drums again?'

His eyebrows went up mockingly before he turned away to comply with her request. She almost expected him to make some derogatory remark about taped atmosphere, but he didn't. She found the native music restful as they sat in the soft light. It was slightly soporific, even—she smiled as she thought it—anaesthetising. It shielded her from thinking too hard, or from being stiff and self-conscious in the planter's company. They had not had any wine and yet she felt ever so slightly intoxicated. From the walls, the long black carved mask with its border of hair and girigiri shells stared down expressionlessly. The bow still leaned in its corner, the fascinating designs on the tapas drew her eyes again and again. All these things were embodiments of this strange land. As, in his own way, was the planter, with his dark gold hair, sitting silent and thoughtful across the small table.

As she put her cup down she turned her palm leaf basket so that she could view its charming curves from another angle. She was aware of Pierce Adams' regard, and now he remarked dryly, 'It was good of Unkapenna to make you such a generous gift of my strawberries, wasn't it? The basket, by the way, is nothing unusual. Palm leaf baskets are made all over the Territory. It won't last. It will lose its lovely greenness, it will dry up, turn brown, and fall to pieces, and you'll be left with a handful of dust.'

Her gaze held his steadily, and she said mildly, 'I know it will fall to pieces. But in the meantime it will have given me a deal of pleasure.'

'Is that your general philosophy on life?'

She frowned and bit her lip, disconcerted. 'What do you mean?'

He shrugged and spread his hands. '*Maski!* We won't pursue it ... Have you seen your Didirman lately?'

The question took her by surprise and she blinked. 'We're going to Kundalufa on Saturday. Alec wants to take me to the native market.'

'You'll enjoy that.' He was leaning forward, his hands on his knees, a cigarette between his fingers. His eyes looked slantingly up at her—mockingly? maliciously? It was hard to tell in the warm orange-coloured light. 'It's a great tourist attraction, but not what you would call exciting. However, I don't suppose you want a diet of unadulterated excitement.'

'No.' She didn't know if he was teasing or jeering.

'And if you're as much in love with the Didirman as you implied the other day——' Now his eyes questioned her, quizzed her, and he waited for her to say something.

She lowered her lashes, reached forward, and nervously took one of the strawberries.

'If you're serious,' he persisted, and now she looked up and quickly away again, his eyes were so intent.

'Yes, I am serious.' She spoke huskily. 'I wouldn't have come all this way otherwise, would I?'

'Wouldn't you? No, I suppose you wouldn't have ... Well then, you'll enjoy yourself wherever he takes you. To date,' he went on slowly and deliberately, 'he doesn't appear to have been overwhelmingly attentive, does he?'

She flushed at his implication. 'That's because of his work—he's not free.'

'You don't think he could be free if it suited him?'

She widened her eyes. 'Of course not!'

'Perhaps you're right.' He stood up abruptly. 'Come on and I'll tell you about some of my odds and ends.'

She left her chair relievedly, and he showed her a stone axe fashioned from grey-green stone. It was beautifully shaped and the handle was bound on with cane.

'This is from the Jimi River. Such things are becoming rare, now that steel axes are to be bought. Soon they'll be museum pieces.' He showed her next a ceremonial hook carved from wood, crude yet beautiful. She could see the shape of two hornbills, one of them upside down so that the great curved beak made a hook. He left her turning it over in her hands and admiring the primitive workmanship, and came back a moment later with what he said was one of his most valued possessions. It was a magnificent feathered headdress, presented to him by the *luluai* of some Highland village, though Pierce did not tell her what the occasion had been. Parma touched it reverently, newly aware of the native music throbbing hauntingly in the background. She knew this was a magnificent gift, and she wondered deeply about the man who had received it. The feathers sprang from a single curved piece of shell—a *mainduma*—which was mounted on a deep band of soft beaten bark, painted with geometric irregular designs in red and black. Crimson parrot quills were backed by huge sprays of red-gold Paradise plumes of incredible splendour, and from them cascaded long streamers of satiny black tail feathers. It was barbaric and beautiful, and Parma could not help thinking of the birds that had been slaughtered for its creation.

'It's against the law to take these feathers out of the country,' Pierce told her. 'And it goes without saying that the Bird of Paradise is protected from European hunters. So don't go coveting anything like this or wondering if you will manage to take home even a single feather, for you won't,' he finished, half banteringly.

'I wouldn't want to,' said Parma gravely. 'Besides——'

'Besides what?' He stood close and he was smiling

down at her, and she reflected with surprise that she had been strangely at her ease with him this evening, all things considered.

'Besides, I think these feathers belong here, with the people and the jungle. It would be a sort of—desecration to take them away—out of their context.'

'I agree. You're quite right.' He turned suddenly away from her. *'Em husat, ia?'*

Parma had not heard a sound but, incredibly, Alec stood in the doorway, and swift colour flooded her cheeks, then drained away again.

'Hello, Pierce. Hello, Parma—looks like you live here these days. Can you spare a moment for me?'

'Take her along, Alec,' Pierce said. He looked displeased and his voice was hard. 'I was amusing your girl with some of my collection. I'm sure she's seen quite enough of it.'

Parma was almost too confused to thank him properly for her dinner and the music. She put her scarf around her shoulders and started towards Alec, who still stood in the doorway, hands on hips, smiling slightly.

'You're forgetting your strawberries.' Pierce spoke dryly and she turned quickly, nearly bumping into him. When she took the basket his fingers touched hers and she knew a sense of shock. She was thoroughly unnerved by the time she had got away from the bungalow.

Alec had lit a cigarette and didn't take her arm as they went through the garden. A single light shone from the Barlows' and their car was not there so she knew they were not yet home.

'So this is what you do when my back is turned,' Alec said jokingly, kicking at a stone with the toe of his heavy boot. 'You spend your time making love to the planter, do you?'

'Of course I don't, Alec,' she said hotly. 'I hardly ever see him. But Helen and David were out tonight

90

and——'

'All right, all right, darling,' he interrupted her. 'No need to go on, I was only joking. I don't think Pierce Adams would find you particularly to his liking. I'm sure it was a very innocent evening.'

'Yes, it was.'

'Well, it can continue innocent,' he told her laconically. 'I'm not staying longer than five minutes. I'm tired and I'm filthy, and I'm on my way back to the station. I only stopped in to let you know that I've got to spend tomorrow in Kundalufa. The boss has called a conference. I shall have to stay the night, which means you must make your own arrangements for getting in to town on Saturday. Think you can manage it?'

Parma's heart sank. 'I don't know——'

'Well, make an effort, won't you, darling? We haven't seen all that much of each other and time's getting short.'

Was it? Was that the way he saw her visit? She felt pain and a dull shock. 'I will try, Alec. I'll ask Helen what I can do.'

'Fine. I'll meet you at the market, then, some time during the morning.' He put one arm around her and hugged her to him. His body felt hot despite the cool night air and she bit her lip. 'I shan't kiss you—I really am filthy. But we'll make up for it on Saturday. We'll stay the night at the Bird. Okay?'

'I'll look forward to it, Alec.'

She could hardly believe it when he had roared off in his jeep and she was alone. She couldn't go back to Pierce's bungalow now, and she felt regret that her evening had been broken into—for nothing. She had felt a faint sense of triumph just at first after Alec arrived, because it had shown the planter that her Didirman did get in to see her sometimes. Now she was left with a problem on her hands: how to get in to Kundalufa on Saturday.

Her evening was thoroughly spoilt, and a little

phrase Alec had used nagged and nagged at her mind. 'Time's getting short.'

She went slowly into the bungalow and in her room sat down and ate two of Pierce's strawberries. In the morning, she thought, the basket will be beginning to wither. Well, there would be other baskets—other strawberries...

She went into Kundalufa with Pierce. He was going, she understood from Helen, to attend a business meeting with Jim Loveday, the manager of his copra plantation on the north coast. It was lucky for Parma because the Barlows were off to a village where the Garfields had told her she would find an old native with a fount of folk tales.

Parma and Pierce were both quiet during the drive. Parma supposed that the planter's mind was full of the business talk ahead of him and she did not want to bother him with chatter. The other night, she had felt almost at ease with him, but today he was aloof and withdrawn, and she had the distinct feeling that he was not at all impressed that Alec had left her to get into Kundalufa on her own. She was not sorry when at last he dropped her off outside the native market.

'Sure you'll be all right?' he asked casually.

'Yes, of course—Alec will be there.'

'Enjoy yourself.' He drove off, leaving her alone in the heat of the morning.

She stood looking about her in some bewilderment. The market was held in a great open space on the edge of the town, shaded by feathering casuarinas and palms. There was an astonishing crowd milling about, a mixture of Europeans and New Guineans, with the latter predominating. They in their turn were a mixture of Europeanised town dwellers in conventional clothing and villagers from the hills in native dress— some wearing next to nothing, some decked out more exotically in arrays of feathers and shells. Three long sheds with open sides and thatched roofs sheltered long tables where goods for sale were laid out, and round about, other indigenes squatted on the ground, their wares spread around them. Near where she stood, Parma saw a native girl sitting cross-legged before a pile of *kaukau*, passion-fruit, and sugar cane. She wore several strings of bright trade-store beads and an apron of tanked leaves, unreal in their pinks and purples and yellows.

Parma stood on the fringe of the crowd for several minutes, hoping she might see Alec, but soon she couldn't resist going in. Little boys offered strings of black-seed beads hopefully, and she bought some—bronze and ivory-coloured, very light in weight—for ten cents, and put them around her neck. The sun was burning hot and she headed for the shade of the thatched sheds.

It was an excitingly colourful market and the stall-holders were the most fascinating part of all—they and the native customers. It was an odd sensation to find oneself rubbing shoulders with the near-naked women, who had *bilums* tied high on their foreheads in a top-knot, and hanging down their backs like a cloak, and otherwise wore no dress but a fringe of grass, some beads, or an armband or two. There was a table where meat was sold; there were bundles of beans or carrots tied up with grass; there was *kaukau* galore, cobs of corn, pumpkins, cucumbers and tomatoes; passion-fruit and pawpaws, melons and pineapples, bunches of green bananas; there were citrus fruits—called *muli*, be they lemons, oranges, or grapefruit—and bundles of sugar cane. There was a woman with a pot of dough, a pot of boiling oil, and a bundle of sticks, and Parma stood watching as she dipped a stick into the thick dough, twirled it around deftly, then plunged it into the oil. It looked repulsive when it emerged, Parma thought, yet the indigenes were buying it and eating it with relish.

She looked up from her contemplation of this weird kind of fairy floss, and suddenly, in a cleared space, she saw Pierce Adams with a very young, very blonde girl. Her heart lurched.

She had thought, for some reason, that he was immune to the charms of women, but he stood looking down at this girl almost tenderly, his hand on her arm. And he had said he was going to Kundalufa on business! Quickly, Parma turned away before he could see her. She wished that Alec were there and began to wonder how they could possibly find each other. Almost without thinking, she took up a bundle of sugar cane, and the native woman smiled and lisped, 'Ten cen.' Ten cents. Parma fished in her purse and brought out two five-cent pieces. The woman shook her head emphatically. '*Nogat!*' What did she mean? Parma was bewildered. 'This is ten cents.' She tried to press the coins on the woman and a little hubbub arose around her. She couldn't think why her money should be unacceptable.

Then suddenly Pierce Adams was there, he had handed over a ten-cent piece and everything, quite ludicrously, was in order.

'What did I do wrong?' asked Parma, puzzled and aware of her heightened colour.

'You offered five-cent pieces,' said Pierce with a humorous look. 'To a lot of them, that's not the same at all. Didn't Alec warn you to stock up well with ten-cent pieces?' The blonde girl stood a little behind him and stared openly at Parma. Her eyes were very blue and heavily lashed and they did not smile at all. Parma felt vaguely uncomfortable under her gaze. Then Pierce turned slightly and drew the girl forward. 'This is Sophie Gide, Parma. Sophie—Miss Parma Drew. As you probably know, she's staying with the Barlows for a while.'

Sophie did no more than murmur, but still she stared and Parma began to wonder if there were something odd about her own get-up—the beads, perhaps? She fingered them nervously and said, 'How do you do?' Somehow, it seemed impossible to say in a friendly way, 'I've heard of you,' because the other girl looked so moody and sullen and stared so rudely. What had Helen said? 'She's just a child.' Well, she was a child who had not learned manners, thought Parma, unnerved, but she remarked determinedly, 'It's a very colourful market, that's for sure. But I don't like my chances of finding Alec. I suppose you haven't seen him, Pierce?'

Pierce said no, he hadn't, and Sophie stopped staring and muttered that she had to meet her brother. Without even a word of goodbye, she hurried away and disappeared into the crowd. Parma looked at Pierce in amazement, but his eyes were hard and unresponsive.

'I hope I haven't broken anything up,' she said coolly.

'Not at all. I see you've bought yourself some beads,' he said. 'Have you seen the *bilums* yet?' Evidently Sophie's precipitate departure was to pass without comment. He took her arm lightly and led her towards one of the other sheds where net bags were displayed. They had a single handle and were made from a rather harsh-feeling coloured string.

'The women make the string themselves from tree fibres,' Pierce told Parma. 'They roll it on their thighs to form long cords, then colour it with dyes from plants. Though nowadays, of course, they've increased their colour range with trade store dyes.'

Parma fingered the *bilums* interestedly. Some were enormous, others were little more than handbag size, and the patterns were asymmetrical and pleasing to the eye.

'You'll have to bargain for a price,' Pierce said. 'You can expect to pay up to ten or twelve dollars.'

Parma didn't think she would be able to afford so

much, but refrained from comment. She was thinking still of Sophie Gide who had been so strangely unfriendly, and she felt vaguely sorry for her. Her family background was sad enough and now the plantation was apparently far from paying its way ... She put down the *bilum* she had been holding and looked up at Pierce.

'What happened about the men you sent to work on the Kunai Valley Estate?'

'They haven't begun yet. The *singsing*'s just over. But Monday they'll be there ... See anything you like?'

'I haven't made up my mind.' She wished that Alec would come. She was sure Pierce didn't want to hang around here with her—he would probably have gone with Sophie to meet her brother but for Parma. She said at last, 'Don't bother staying with me, Pierce. I shall be all right and Alec will be here any minute now.'

'I'll wait until he comes,' said Pierce briefly, and it was not long after that he spotted Alec. He was at an advantage as he towered over the heads of most of the people milling around the stalls. 'Here's your Didirman now, so I'll be on my way. I have a date in half an hour.'

A date! Parma watched him walk quickly out into the sunlight, saw it burning gold on his hair. That was hardly the way one would refer to a business appointment. She wondered if his date was with Sophie Gide. She was beginning to think that Pierce had a secret life of his own, once he was away from Butterfly Montane...

Alec had caught sight of her now and raised his hand in greeting.

'Hello, darling.' He stopped and kissed her lightly and automatically took the small overnight bag she was carrying. She felt relieved that he had not seen Pierce. She was not in the mood for any more jokes about her association with the planter. 'I thought I

96

might find you hovering over the *bilum* display. It always seems to fascinate the girls. Have you picked the one you would like yet?'

'There is one I particularly like, but I'm afraid it may cost too much.' She indicated a bag of medium size in colours of orange, blue and natural. 'I don't know how to ask the price.'

'*Haumas?*' Alec didn't seem to waste time in bargaining and before she realised it he had handed over some notes and the *bilum* was hers. 'There, that's a present. Sure you like it?'

'Oh, Alec, I love it! But I didn't mean you to buy it for me.' She didn't know why, but she felt oddly guilty accepting the gift. And yet she had let him buy her an opal ring, which was much more personal and much more valuable, without a qualm. Had the situation between them changed so much that she felt as she did? Troubled, she hung the gay net bag over her arm and put the small bundle of sugar cane in it.

'What else would you like?' Alec took her hand in his and they wandered along the stalls. There were armbands and waistbands made of seeds and trade store beads and fibre, and Alec chose a bracelet of red and green and yellow beads arranged in a diamond pattern. Then he bought her a little spray of tanked leaves and flowers to tuck into it. It looked pretty against her yellow sleeveless dress, and the flowers smelt sweet, and soon she became quite caught up in the gaiety and novelty of the market—the excitement of bright things, the pleasure of being able to express her delight to someone. Alec introduced her to several Europeans doing their Saturday morning shopping— administration workers and their wives, a couple of teachers, a Kiap on a brief visit to town. Mostly they were followed by a *hausboi* who was carrying their greengrocery purchases, and some of them had small children with them.

Alec took her to the Bird of Paradise Hotel for lunch,

and as she freshened up in the powder room, and as she stood back from the mirror to admire her beaded armband and the flowers, still fresh and stiff and sweet, she wondered if they would encounter Pierce and Sophie Gide in the dining room. She rather hoped not.

Luck was with her. Some of the people she had met at the market were there, and she was introduced to one or two other people. A bit of banter was exchanged, and Alec was complimented more than once on his pretty girl-friend.

Parma's cheeks grew flushed. She was enjoying her day out! Alec planned to take her to the Haus Blanket after lunch.

'I'll buy you a poncho—I don't think you need a rug or a blanket.'

'Definitely not,' she laughed. 'I don't *really* need a poncho either, Alec.'

'Of course you do! The nights are cool, and you can't come to New Guinea without buying one of our ponchos.' He was holding her hand as they left the dining room together, and she had a happy feeling that they were at last getting back on to their old footing. Alec seemed much more like the warm companion she had known in Sydney. He had booked her a room in the hotel, her small case had already been sent up, and now a neatly dressed New Guinean showed her to it, for she had decided to change her shoes while Alec waited on the terrace. Parma was entranced with her room. Last time she had been here—what a long time ago it seemed to be!—she had been in too much of a turmoil to enjoy her surroundings. Now she took a keen delight in the pretty cane furniture, the blue and green bed quilt and curtains with their striking native designs. She hung up the long cotton dress she had brought with her—a fine voile in black and white— and brushed out her hair at the mirror. She changed into sturdier shoes and stared at herself in the mirror as though she were a stranger. Her pale cheeks were delicately flushed and her hair was at its prettiest and silkiest. She thought she did not look bad at all—though she wished not for the first time that she were a little taller and that her figure was not quite so slender.

Before she went down to rejoin Alec she stepped out on to the narrow balcony with its green awning. It was a beautiful day, perhaps a little too hot, but there would be relief at sundown. Above in a pale blue sky big white clouds floated and beyond the small town the dark line of mountains was softened by a tumble of mist. As she glanced down at the terrace to pick out Alec, she saw Pierce Adams' car pull up. He climbed out of it and a girl got out of the other side. It was not Sophie Gide. It was a tall young woman with a beautifully tanned skin and thick brown hair piled up on top of her head in a careless knot. She wore an exotic-looking ivory-coloured dress with a brilliantly embroidered panel down the front, at the hem, and on the edges of the elbow-length sleeves. She walked with Pierce into the hotel, her arm through his, her head held proudly.

Parma went rather slowly back into her room. *That* girl was no tourist—no outsider. She was a true Territorian if ever there was one—it showed in every lovely, healthy, assured inch of her. Who was she? Parma thought she had been a fool to imagine that there were no women in Pierce's life because he had been jilted once. A man of his obvious virility, with his striking appearance and air of command, would never be left alone by women—would never want to be left alone. It was only girls who reminded him of Rowena Arnold —girls like Parma—that he would steer clear of.

Parma looked in the mirror and now she was dissatisfied with what she saw. She was pale—insignificant—— She turned away, took up her new net bag, and left the room, slamming the door behind her.

What was the matter with her that she felt so suddenly out of tune with the world? Downstairs Alec was waiting for her; that should be enough to make her feel happy for a start. They were all set for a visit to the Haus Blanket, they had a dinner and dance ahead of them—for Alec had promised to take her to the Kundalufa Sports Club—and tomorrow was Sunday, which meant that Alec would again be free all day. So everything was fine, she told herself firmly, and hurried across the terrace towards him.

'What a time you've been!' he reproached her. 'Never mind—you look very sweet. You're worth waiting for.'

'Am I, Alec?'

'Aren't I always telling you so? Why do you think I took such a fancy to you in Sydney? Not because you're an ugly little duckling, that's for sure.... Now hop into the jeep and we'll be on our way.'

The Haus Blanket was out in the hills, and though today no weaving was in progress, goods were on sale and there was a continual stream of cars bringing Europeans to look and to buy. Parma found she could pick out the tourists. They carried cameras and they were more fussily dressed, and the women wore more make up than the expatriate Europeans. She wondered if she looked like a tourist, with her spanking new *bilum* and her beaded armband, and she supposed a little sadly that she did. Maybe she was just that—a tourist.

'Alec, do I look like a tourist?' she asked as they left the jeep.

'You look like a holidaymaker.' Alec patted her arm and she was not consoled. She wanted more than humouring from Alec. After all, she had come here with a serious purpose, believing that he wanted to consolidate the relationship that had grown up between them in Sydney. Had she been over-optimistic? Had she read too much into his seemingly enthusiastic invitation? Was Pierce right when he implied that

Alec could be seeing a lot more of her if he wished to?

Resolutely she put Pierce Adams out of her thoughts. She was here with Alec now and she was going to make the most of it . . .

They went into one of the big sheds where the looms were housed, and there they saw rugs and blankets, some still on the looms and only partly made, others complete and rolled up against the walls or spread out on display. Some were plain cream or brown, others were irregularly striped like the floor rugs in Pierce's bungalow. They were very thick and heavy and, watching an Australian couple who were selecting one, Parma realised that they were sold by weight. They wandered around for a while so that she could see the rugs, then Alec took her arm.

'I'm afraid I can't get very excited over this stuff. Come along and we'll find the ponchos.' He took her across neatly cropped grass surrounded by beds of cannas and into a smaller shed where the ponchos were for sale. They were diamond-shaped, very simple with a slit in the middle; more finely woven than the rugs and made in reds and greens and browns. Some were big enough to reach to the ground on a tall person, others were tiny enough for little children. With Alec's help, Parma chose a red one for herself. It had a touch of darkest brown here and there, and Alec said it set off her colouring—her fair skin and shining dark hair.

Alec handed it over to the New Guinean attendant, in laplap and shirt, to be weighed and priced.

'*Em i gutpela samting. Pei bilong en haumas?*'

The poncho—the 'something'—was weighed and money changed hands, and again Parma felt an uneasy embarrassment about the gift. But Alec's brown eyes smiled down at her. 'Wear it tonight and I'll be proud of you. Now, have you seen enough?'

But Parma had spotted a tiny red poncho and she could picture Elisabet in it. She took it to the native salesman. *'Haumas dispela samting?'*

He gave her a grin, weighed it up, told her, *'Tri dolla.'* In a moment it was hers.

'Who's it for? A favourite niece?' Alec wanted to know.

She shook her head. 'It's for Elisabet—Pierce's *hausboi's* little girl.'

'Good lord,' was all Alec said.

But Parma felt more pleased and excited about that tiny *'samting'* than she had felt about anything else all day.

When she dressed in her hotel room at sundown, she draped her own red poncho over her arm. It looked well with her long black and white dress—gave it a lift. She had been tempted to pin up her hair, but she knew Alec liked it loose, so she wore it down.

It was incredibly chilly outside. The sky was filled with cloud and by the time they reached the Sports Club on a sloping hill at the other end of the town, the sun had disappeared entirely and lights were shining everywhere. In the big dining room with its small dance floor at one end soft taped music was playing. Long windows opened on to a terrace ornamented with ferns and palm and orchids growing in huge stone pots. Down below was the sports field, and beyond, twinkling lights shone from the scattered houses of the small administration town.

A New Guinean waiter showed them to a table and as she seated herself she saw in the soft lamplight several people whom she had met during the day. It gave her a warm feeling to see hands raised in greeting, smiles of recognition all around. It was another good moment and she looked across at Alec. Tonight, apart from the beard, he looked much more like the Alec she felt she really knew. He wore a light tropical suit and his dark hair was smooth and well groomed. She gave a little sigh and settled back in her chair. Over dinner they would have a long and intimate talk, and then they would dance and he would hold her close. Everything was going to work out all right. She touched the opal ring on her right hand and thought of the gifts Alec had bought her during the day. She was crazy to have felt guilty about them. He wouldn't have spent all that money on her unless——

'What are you thinking about?' He was leaning forward to smile at her. 'You're going off into one of your dreams! Time to wake up and take a look at the menu.'

She became aware that the waiter was presenting it to her, and as she took it she saw over the top of it two people waiting near the entrance to be shown to a table—Pierce and the tall girl with the brown hair.

Her heart gave a sickening thud and Alec turned his head, following her gaze.

'Shall we ask Pierce and his girl-friend to join us?'

Surely he couldn't have said that! She looked at him uncomprehendingly, a wild feeling of panic growing within her. She wanted to have Alec to herself. She didn't want anyone to join them—particularly not Pierce Adams and that girl, whoever she might be. But Alec, apparently not even contemplating the fact that she might have any objections to his proposal, was not looking at her. His eyes were still on the couple across the room.

'That's Glenda Loveday. I've met her once or twice. Her father runs Pierce's copra plantation at the coast. Hang on, Parma—I'll see how they feel about joining us.'

Parma watched him go with a sinking heart. She could feel her pulses pounding, and the blood throbbed at her temples like the throbbing of distant kundu drums. With all her being she willed Pierce Adams to say no. And yet when she saw him coming towards the table with Alec she knew an almost overpowering sense of inevitability.

CHAPTER SEVEN

'WELL, this is very pleasant,' said Pierce, looking down at Parma. His hair shone dull gold, and he looked wildly exciting in his dark lounge suit, a glint of derisive humour in his strange eyes. 'Let me introduce you —Glenda, this is Parma Drew, our little visitor from— where shall I say, Parma? Is it from England, or have you settled in Australia?' He didn't wait for her to reply but continued smoothly, 'This is Glenda Loveday who's flown in from the coast for a business talk.'

A business talk! Surely the sardonic undertones in his voice made nonsense of that! The two girls smiled at each other, and Pierce held a chair for Glenda. Close up, she looked older than Parma had at first thought—she wouldn't be far off thirty, Parma guessed, though those very fine lines around her eyes could be part of the price one pays for living in the tropics. She wore next to no make-up, but there was a glow of vitality in her hazel eyes, and she had a beautiful mouth with generous curves that were only faintly sensual. She wore a long dress of orange vermilion, a batik print, its lines almost straight so that the utmost was made of the lovely original material with its orange and black border at the hem and across the wide straight neckline. Her only ornament was a single earring—a silver chain from which hung a small bird carved from wood. It looked like the work of some native craftsman, and was both unusual and exclusive. Parma felt vaguely overawed, and very conscious of the fact that this girl was exactly right for Pierce Adams. She would fit into the background of the bungalow at Butterfly Montane with no trouble at all.

'Let's order, shall we?' They were all seated and the waiter hovered.

Parma hardly knew what they ate. She let Alec order for her and somehow she dealt fairly adequately with her dinner, though she found she was not really hungry despite her day in the open air. She sipped without really tasting it the sparkling pink wine that Glenda had chosen and everyone had agreed to. It was all quite glamorous. The lights were soft and flattering, there were orchids on the table, and, contrastingly, a couple of stark Sepik ceremonial masks on the nearest wall—a reminder that this was a primitive land as well as being one of tropical beauty.

The conversation had swung quickly away from personal trivialities to a more or less serious discussion of some of the economic and agricultural problems facing the Highlanders. It was a subject that seemed to interest Glenda Loveday intensely, for she asked question after question of Pierce and Alec, and made quick and acute observations of her own, with much reference to the situation on the coast and in the islands. Parma, hopelessly out of her depth, contented herself with listening. It took her next to no time to appreciate the fact that Glenda Loveday was not only lovely to look at, but very intelligent as well, a fact which made her all the more conscious of her own colourlessness and insignificance.

It was pretty plain that her own evening was spoilt. It was not proceeding according to plan at all. She and Alec were not going to talk of love, to remember their first meeting, to discover new things about each other as they looked into one another's eyes to a background of soft music. In fact, the dinner table conversation was developing more and more into a dialogue between two people—Alec and Glenda. Parma, stealing a quick glance at Pierce, found him leaning back lazily, a tolerant half-smile on his good-looking face, as he listened idly to the repartee. He must be very, very sure of Glenda, she mused, to let someone else take her over as Alec was doing. But then they were only talking about such things as an experimental pyrethrum crop, or the problems attached to taking Highland men away from their villages and families for a two-year term on a coastal plantation. It was hardly what one would call a personal or intimate conversation! Parma could not help wondering if Alec would have been so willingly involved had Glenda been middle-aged and plain. He was not always so willing to talk about matters connected with his work!

She became suddenly aware that Pierce was leaning towards her.

'How did your day go, Parma? Did you enjoy yourself at the native market?' His regard was watchful, astute. Was he looking for signs of her reaction to the turn events were taking, wondering if she was as sure of Alec as he was of Glenda? She managed a smile.

'Yes, thank you. We had great fun. Alec bought me a *bilum*—and a bracelet.' She was disconcerted by the analytical way he was watching her, and took up her wine glass nervously. Those eyes were relentless. How did they see her? she wondered. As a silly little creature who was easily entertained by something as tourist-slanted as a native market; small, too thin, colourless in her black and white dress despite the softening warmth of the pink shaded lights; her dark eyes smudged by tiredness, her mouth too wide for her small face. Not, in fact, very impressive—particularly in this company.

'And this afternoon?' Pierce prompted after a pause that seemed to last a lifetime and was filled with the sound of Glenda's positive but pleasantly low-pitched voice saying emphatically, 'I should very much like to meet your anthropologist, Alec, if he's been to all the places you say. What are my chances? I hope to be in the Highlands for a week or two at least.'

'This afternoon,' said Parma, lashes lowered, twirling her wine glass, 'we went to the Haus Blanket.'

'And there Alec bought you the poncho that's now

draped over the back of your chair.'

'Yes. Do you think I'm behaving like the perfect tourist?' She tilted her chin and slanted him a defiant smile.

The corner of his mouth twitched. '*Aiting* . . . At any rate, the colour should suit you. It has a touch of savagery about it and that doesn't come amiss sometimes.' Now she felt he was mocking again and, disquieted, she glanced across at Glenda, glowing in her orange vermilion, intent on her conversation with Alec. Savagery might be a word one could connect with a girl like that—but not with Parma Drew.

'Did Alec tell you anything as prosaic as the fact that we haven't been able to raise sheep here and that our wool is imported from Australia?'

'No,' she admitted. 'But I wondered about it.'

'Did you?' He appeared to consider that for a minute. When he went on the trace of mockery had gone from his eyes and he was quite serious. 'The Haus Blanket is something in the nature of an experiment. It's sponsored by the government and run by Europeans who are teaching the local people to work there and, eventually, how to run the place. The workers buy the wool, make their goods, and sell them back to the government. In my opinion, the one thing missing is artistic direction. But I imagine you were aware of that lack yourself?'

'Yes,' she said diffidently. She was enormously pleased to have him talk to her so sensibly and so seriously, and she waited for him to go on, which he did after a slight pause.

'Learning new ways to make cash is important here. Once, the indigene depended for his wealth very largely on bride prices. So if a man had several wives, he also had quite a pile of gold lip shell, or Paradise plumes or whatever. Now he can have only one wife and become quite wealthy—if he's prepared to cultivate coffee trees or peanuts, for instance.' He brought the fingers of his two hands together and looked at her penetratingly over them, and Parma thought that in many ways this was the oddest evening she had ever spent. But she found she could not look away from him, her eyes were drawn to his magnetically and in his own she could see nothing but a deep and utter seriousness. He asked her softly, 'Am I boring you?'

'No—no—I'm truly interested.' Suddenly she realised that the other two had stopped talking. Their coffee was there and Glenda, reaching for the sugar, said with a friendly smile, 'Then you must try to get over to the coast before you leave us. It's very different from the Highlands, and you'll love Lae, which is very, very pretty and fresh. The town was completely destroyed during the war, you see, and so everything is reasonably new. Perhaps you will come back with me when I go.'

'Thank you,' murmured Parma. She glanced at Alec for his approval or otherwise, but with something of a shock she realised that he was, at this minute, scarcely aware of her. All his attention, warm and intent, was for Glenda.

For a moment she was completely at a loss, and then she told herself that any man would admire a girl as beautiful and intelligent as Glenda Loveday. It was a perfectly natural reaction. But all the same, something in Alec's expression had shocked her deeply, and when he murmured, 'Come and dance,' she looked to him eagerly. But his hand was on Glenda's arm and she drew back, biting her lip, her cheeks white. She knew that Pierce had seen her mistake, and she did her best to hide her hurt by forcing a smile as the other two moved on to the dance floor.

Pierce said nothing. He stood up and held out his hand to her and she took it blindly. She was shattered by what was happening. It was, in a way, more frightening than what had happened to her up in the mountains when her car went off the road and she didn't know what to do. The dream world she had built seemed ready to crumble around her....

She didn't know how long it was before she realised she was standing on the dance floor with Pierce, and he was holding her closely and rocking her rhythmically, gently. Her white dress glowed a soft pink from a lamp overhead—everything was ludicrously rosy, and the music was honey-sweet. She had suffered this kind of mental blackout once before—the evening she read the stark simple letter from William Cunningham, telling her he was going away with her girl-friend. Then, there had been no one to hold her in his arms and rock her. As she realised that Pierce Adams was doing just that, she drew in her breath and pulled a little away from him.

'What's the matter? Did I tread on your toe?' His words were so prosaic and dry that she wondered if her imagination had run away with her. Perhaps there was nothing at all out of the ordinary in the attention that Alec was paying Glenda Loveday—perhaps it was all in her own mind. Then Pierce gathered her to him once more and said, bending his head so that he spoke against her hair, 'I shouldn't worry, little Miss Drew. Your Didirman's just caught up temporarily in an old trap—baited with talk of the land he loves. He's been here seven years, you know. He's wedded to this land and he loves to talk of her—to hear her spoken of. He'll come back to you presently. I promise you that.'

He was right. Alec did come back, but Parma wasn't sure whether it was of his own volition or because from then on Pierce himself monopolised Glenda.

'The planter doesn't like anyone else to have a bit of his cake, does he?' Alec remarked a little later as he and Parma were dancing. 'He's very possessive. He was listening to every word Glenda said to me even while he was talking to you. I suppose you haven't heard any talk of his marrying her, have you?'

Parma hadn't, and told herself wearily that she

wished Pierce Adams and Glenda Loveday were miles away. Pierce should never have agreed to join them at their table—but of course, she reflected bitterly, from what she knew of him it was just the kind of thing he would do.

It was getting late when another couple came into the Club and sat at a small table for two well away from the dance floor—a boy and a girl, both fair and blue-eyed with skins that were a soft golden colour. Sophie Gide and, without a doubt, her brother Arthur. Parma, who saw them before any of the other three did, thought they looked curiously young and defenceless. The boy's mouth was set in a hard line and he didn't look around the room at all, but snapped his fingers for a waiter and ordered drinks. Sophie, who was rather drably dressed in black, glanced quickly and almost furtively around while he was occupied with the waiter. Parma was quite certain the girl saw and recognised her, but she gave no sign, no response to Parma's own quick and friendly smile. Her blue gaze flicked over Parma's companions and then went back to her brother.

It was a minute or so later that Pierce spotted them and raised a hand in greeting. He at least was acknowledged by a fleeting smile from Sophie and what was little more than a twist of the lips from Arthur. Glenda turned casually to see who it was that Pierce had recognised, and by that time the brother and sister were once again apparently unconscious of the presence of anyone else in the crowded room.

Glenda stilled her swinging ear-ring. 'Oh, those Gides!' She eyed Alec with sudden amusement. 'I hear you and Arthur were involved in a bit of a fracas at the Club a few weeks ago.'

'News certainly travels,' Alec sounded bored. He reached for an ashtray to mash out his cigarette, and exhaled smoke.

'Won't you tell us about it?' persisted Glenda. 'You were fighting over a girl, I suppose.'

'I wouldn't say that,' said Alec. His mouth had tightened and his eyes were suddenly hard.

'No?' Glenda laughed. 'Then let's hear your explanation for such behaviour, Alec. Come on—out with it!'

Pierce said coolly, 'It was probably a drunken brawl, Glenda, so don't try to make a drama out of it.'

Parma listened perplexed. A drunken brawl! How could Pierce suggest such a thing! Surely he could not be serious. And Glenda—she had practically taken it for granted that the fight was over a girl. Parma's heart was beating hard, and she was waiting tensely for what Alec would say. He sent her one brief unreadable look and saw that she was listening.

'If you must have it,' he said, and he sounded angry, 'the whole thing hinges on the fact that Arthur, as we all know, has a great big complex about his old man. He has the idea that we visit the sins of the fathers upon the children in these parts, and that about sums it up. You've only to say one little word that can be taken as criticism of Richard Gide, and his hackles rise.' He threw out one hand in a futile gesture. 'That's all there is to it.' He smiled without amusement, reached into his pocket for cigarettes, and offered them around. It was quite obvious that he didn't want to say any more, but for some reason Glenda would not leave it alone.

'So Arthur struck the first blow.'

'If you want to put it like that—yes. Arthur took a swing at me and I retaliated.'

'And who knocked out who?'

Alec shrugged. 'I'm heavier than Arthur and I'm tougher. Also I've been around longer. I couldn't help but win.' He looked at Glenda and now he was really smiling. Parma had a horror of violence and she hated the picture that Alec had conjured up, but Glenda—

Glenda would have liked to see that fight. Parma knew it.

Pierce, who had said nothing for minutes, was watching Parma quizzically and she thought he must despise her for the squeamishness that was apparent in her white face. She turned her head away from him, and Alec said, 'Now let's forget about it, shall we?' He exchanged a worldly look with the girl from the copra plantation, and pushed back his chair. 'Come and dance, Parma. That's more to your taste than talk of blood-spilling, isn't it?'

She went into his arms feeling troubled and wishing the evening would end. There were too many things that had to be digested. Over Alec's shoulder she saw Arthur Gide send him a look of burning hatred, and she wondered about Alec's story. She reflected that after all she didn't really know—and she certainly didn't understand—any of these people. She was a complete outsider. Far more was hidden from her than she could ever imagine. And those dark masks, staring down at her from the wall. Just now they had her almost at screaming point. They were enough to give her nightmare. She shuddered slightly and closed her eyes, and Alec said at once, 'You're tired. I think we'll break it up.'

'Yes, please.' She went ahead of him from the dance floor back to where Pierce and Glenda sat talking. She wrapped the red poncho around herself and said goodnight.

'We'll let you two get on with your business talk,' said Alec with a grin, and in another minute or two he and Parma were out in the cold night air. The sky was misted with cloud, there was not a star to be seen and it had been raining. Parma shivered and Alec put his arm around her. But now she was alone with him her feeling of not really knowing him was stronger than ever. Instead of deepening her understanding of him, her visit to the Highlands seemed to have put a great gulf between them.

He drove fast down the long hill and into the town and when he had pulled up in front of the hotel, he turned to take her in his arms. In less than a moment she was trying to disentangle herself from his embrace. She was too much at variance with him in her mind to deal with his passionate kisses.

'Please, Alec—not now.'

She heard his sigh of exasperation. 'All right.' He flung open the door and when she joined him did not take her arm but kept her distance as they went into the hotel.

'Did you enjoy your day?' He sounded rough and uncaring.

'Yes, thank you. It was very nice.' Her voice ws scarcely audible.

'Well, I suggested you should come here, didn't I? So it's up to me to show you some of the high spots.'

He might just as well have added, thought Parma, 'And it's up to you to be more co-operative.'

Later she lay wakeful in the bed in her hotel room, restless, overtired, her mind plagued by the thought of how determined she had been to escape from Alec's kisses. The day that she had looked forward to so eagerly had certainly ended in disaster! She had been more shocked than she had liked to admit to herself by the way Alec had looked at Glenda Loveday. In another world—another time—he had looked at *her* with that deep and single-minded absorption, and now she was unhappily aware of how far her own looks and personality fell short of those of the girl from the coast—the true Territorian.

Bitterest memory of all, Pierce Adams had felt it incumbent upon him to come to her rescue.

Two men, two girls. But it was Glenda Loveday who had fascinated both the Didirman and the planter.

On this wry thought she fell asleep and dreamed of

Pierce Adams. She was back at Butterfly Montane, giving the little red poncho to Elisabet—watching while the planter lifted the tiny child in his arms and laughed into her laughing face as he swung her high ...

When she went downstairs to breakfast next morning, Alec was already there, and Parma's heart sank as she saw that Pierce and Glenda sat at the table with him. The men stood up as she came in and Glenda sent her a lazy welcoming smile. Another woman might have commented cattily on Parma's appearance, for she had not slept well and her eyes were smudged by dark shadows that she had not been able to hide. But Glenda had nothing unkind to say—'This grapefruit is delicious! You must have some, Parma.' Not by so much as a blink did she betray any awareness of the fact that Parma looked completely washed out. Perhaps, Parma found herself thinking, she did not even notice it.

Pierce, in fact, was the only one to comment, and that was later while the other two were talking. Then he leaned across and asked her with faint derision, 'Did your Didirman keep you up late, Parma? You must be out of training when it comes to high living.'

Parma flashed him a look of hatred. She wished he would keep out of her life and stop interfering. At that moment it seemed to her to be all his fault that everything was going wrong. He had wished it on her from the very beginning. Yet if she and Alec had been left alone yesterday, everything would have been quite different. Her spirits sank still lower when Glenda asked cheerfully,

'What are you two doing today?'

'What do you suggest?' Alec asked.

Glenda flung out her elegant hands. 'Has Parma had enough of sightseeing? What about a drive out to the river? Everyone goes there on Sundays.'

'Will *you* be going there?' Alec, smiling, wanted to know.

'We're making a move,' said Pierce drawlingly. He pushed back his chair. 'We're leaving for the plantation in half an hour or so.'

Relief flooded Parma's being. She wouldn't have those two to contend with today! And yet the thought of a whole day alone with Alec was now more than a little daunting. She heard Pierce saying dryly, 'You'll see Parma gets home safely, won't you, Alec?'

'Yes, of course. Leave it to me.' He sounded thoughtful.

When the others had gone, Parma was somehow not surprised to hear Alec say, 'You know, I think I've had about enough of Kundalufa too. I think we'll make a move as well.'

'Could we go to Varmari, Alec?' Parma asked it so quickly she was hardly aware of having thought of it.

'Varmari? There's not a thing to do at the station. No, I'm going to take you back to Butterfly Montane. You look like a half-drowned kitten today—in no condition to be dragged around sightseeing. We'll see what's doing when we get to the plantation.'

Parma knew with a dry throat and a terrible certainty that it was because of Glenda that they were going to the plantation. Worse still, Pierce would know it too.

After breakfast she went upstairs to pack her things. She dabbed at the dark shadows under her eyes with liquid make-up, then gave up in despair. Suddenly she thought with relief of getting back to the Barlows' bungalow. She would be able to relax in her room—to talk to Helen—to give Pawpaw the tiny poncho for Elisabet. She could imagine the laughing pride in Unkapenna's face when he saw his little daughter...

She was feeling quite cheerful when she rejoined Alec and they set off in the jeep. His spirits were high too, and the long drive passed happily enough, the only odd thing being that they never once discussed anything serious. But Parma was getting used to that now. In fact, she no longer really expected it.

Driving between the shadowy casuarinas and the dark coffee trees was like coming home. Parma felt all the tension leave her as she looked about her eagerly. She had the funny feeling that her ears were almost pricked—waiting for the magic of the vibrating gong that was *belo*. But it was Sunday, and there was no *belo* today. As she climbed from the jeep outside the Barlows' bungalow, she breathed deeply, filling her nostrils with the scent of the yellow ginger blossoms. Alec said, 'Nip in with your *kago*, Parma—it's not more than you can manage, is it? Tell the Barlows you're back and I'll see what's doing at Pierce's. They'll be surprised to see us here!'

Parma bit her lip. But she was crazy to make anything of it. It was just that Alec liked company. When she thought about the fun they had had in Sydney— most of the time they had been in the midst of a crowd. And Alec's ability to talk to absolutely anyone, to make a party of it even when they had gone to some place on their own had never ceased to amaze her. She had admired him for it then, so what was she worrying about? *She* was the one he had invited to New Guinea. Glenda was Pierce's girl, if she could be said to be anyone's, and soon she would be back in Kundalufa.

Her step lightened as she went into the bungalow calling out, 'I'm back, Helen.' She decided not to become introspective or analytical any more. She must take Alec as he was and see what emerged. She would hardly make an impression on anyone if she was sulky and silent and disagreeable.

Helen came from the kitchen to greet her, hugging her like an old friend, and David appeard at the sitting room door where he was fiddling with the record player, which was not performing up to standard. 'Hello, Parma. We missed you.'

Helen, her arm around Parma's waist, accompanied her to her room. 'Did you have a good time in Kundalufa? Wait till you hear my new stories ... Where's Alec?'

'Gone over to Pierce's,' said Parma cheerfully. 'Glenda Loveday has come up for the day. I think Alec's hoping to work up a picnic or something. You know him.'

Helen gave her rather an odd look, a little amused. 'So it was Glenda who flew over to talk business and not Jim. Well, I'm not really surprised ... Now are you going to eat with us? I'm in the process of getting lunch—it's a salad, and I can easily prepare enough for four.'

'You're a darling. I'll see what Alec says.'

She met Alec halfway between the two bungalows.

'Get your bikini, Parma, we're going down to the river pool. The *hausboi*'s packing us up some *kai*.'

It was a very pleasant picnic. Helen and David came down to swim later in the afternoon. Alec was quite charmingly attentive to Parma, and for her part she set herself out to be bright and positive. Glenda, who looked like some goddess in her brown and gold one-piece swimsuit, didn't put herself out to appear anything other than what she was—which was a good deal, for she was a beautiful, intelligent, and sophisticated young woman. It was no wonder Alec admired her! Parma was perfectly aware that all three men did, and she caught each one of them looking admiringly and appreciatively at Glenda at some time or another.

Well, Glenda would soon be gone again from the immediate vicinity. Meanwhile, the sunshine was hot and it was heavenly to lie baking on a smooth flat boulder after playing vigorously in the water for half an hour or so. She would soon be acquiring quite a tan herself.

Parma on her boulder dozed a little and woke as a few drops of cold water splashed on to her bare back.

She sat up and found the planter had hauled himself on to the rock beside her and was looking at her with eyes that missed nothing. With a suddenness that made her colour, she remembered that other day she'd encountered him at the river pool—how he had pulled her against him and his body had been sun-hot and he had kissed her roughly. He was remembering that too, she was sure of it. She stared at him as though mesmerised, her lips parted and her breath coming shallowly. It seemed to her that an age passed before he said, 'Don't stare at me like that. I'm not going to——'

'To kill me and eat me,' she said with a breathless little laugh. She turned her head away and shaded her eyes to look over at the bank where the others were.

'Exactly. I came, in fact, on a peaceful mission. We're packing up. The party's over.'

'Oh. I suppose you'll be driving Glenda back to Kundalufa. Or will you wait till after—*kaikai bilong apinun*?' Back came her eyes, unwilling, yet somehow compelled to meet his own, and he was smiling a little at her attempt at pidgin. She wished he would be merciful and not stare at her the way he did.

'Glenda's here for a holiday,' he said. 'She'll be at the plantation for the next couple of weeks or so.'

'Oh,' she said again. But it was like a flick on a raw place. She bit her lip, looked down at the water and it was dark and cold. She didn't think she could plunge into it again and swim across to the bank. It had been so warm here on her boulder.

Glenda would be here—right here—at the plantation, for the next couple of weeks or so——

The sun went behind a cloud and Pierce looked up. 'It's going to rain this evening... Are you coming? Or do you want us to leave you here all by yourself.'

'I'm coming.' It took an immense effort of will to slide down into the water, and its coldness was an icy shock to her sun-warmed body. Pierce swam lazily at her side and helped her out on the rock they called the landing stage. Alec threw her orange beach towel across to her and she wrapped it around her body, shivering in the scanty yellow bikini.

'You should have brought your lovely poncho,' said Glenda. Parma thought she spoke to her as if she were a child—kindly, unbearably kindly.

'You're blue with cold,' said Helen. 'And it's going to rain.'

Alec came and put his arm around her. He was dressed again in white shorts and checked shirt, his black hair was still wet, and fell across his forehead. 'I'll keep you warm, honey.'

The planter cocked a sardonic eyebrow and turned away, and Parma felt as cold as ever.

She escaped for a few minutes back at the bungalow. The rain had not come yet, and there had been a brilliant and unexpected burst of sunlight. In Unkapenna's small house, Pawpaw was cooking the evening meal, and Elisabet was playing on the grass in her little string skirt. Parma produced the tiny poncho.

'*Mi bringim dispela samting i bilong* Elisabet,' she said slowly and uncertainly.

Pawpaw giggled. '*Yu gutpela misis.*'

Elisabet was running around outside in the red poncho looking so sweet Parma couldn't keep her eyes off her when Pierce came into the garden. She saw him standing, hands on hips, looking at the little brown child running round and round on the grass, her red poncho flying. He caught Parma's eye and his eyebrows went up. Then with a shrug and a grimace, he went away.

'Nothing pleases him—nothing that I do,' thought Parma. And she told herself she didn't care.

Alec stayed to dinner—at the Barlows. When she went outside to see him off, music was drifting over from the other bungalow—a Mozart Violin Concerto. But away in the night, from the hills, Parma could hear the throb and beat of kundu drums. When Alec had gone she stood there, her arms wrapped around herself, shivering in the cold night air. The rain that Pierce had predicted had come—a shower lasting no more than half an hour. The ground was wet, the palms and shrubs glistened with moisture, the ginger blossoms smelt sweet. And behind the civilised music of Mozart, far away and yet so close they were like the pulse of her own blood through her veins, the kundu drums sounded. Parma looked at the little *rum slip* that stood a few yards from Pierce's bungalow. To-night—and for many nights—Glenda Loveday would sleep there.

Well, what of it? What of it?

CHAPTER EIGHT

Now at the plantation everything was subtly different, simply because Glenda Loveday was there. It shouldn't have made a great deal of difference to Parma, and yet it did. Even when she was involved in typing out Helen's stories, fascinating though they were with their backgrounds of mighty river or cloud forest or mountains that went up to the sky, there at the back of her mind always ready to surface and vaguely trouble her, was the thought of Glenda.

From the room where she worked, a small sun room at the end of the verandah, she could look out into the garden and across towards the other bungalow and the small *rum slip* where once Rowena Arnold and now Glenda was accommodated. Often she saw Glenda and the planter walking together, always talking, always close, or she would see them driving off in his Land-Rover. Glenda accompanied him about the estate continually, and it was rarely that he went anywhere at all without her. It caused Parma to speculate on the relationship between them. Was Pierce Adams thinking once more of taking a wife? If he was, and if he had chosen Glenda, then he would certainly not be making the same mistake as he had that other time.

Alec came to the Butterfly Montane on two separate evenings during the first week of Glenda's visit. Each time, he and Parma went to Pierce's bungalow, where they stayed talking and playing records until late, and Alec finally decided he must get back to Varmari. It was very obvious now that he was attracted to Glenda, and yet Parma didn't think he was seriously falling in love with her. As for the older girl, she certainly enjoyed talking to Alec, but then she was a woman who invariably enjoyed talking to members of the opposite

121

sex, particularly those with whom she had common interests. It was Pierce whom she most admired, of course. Discussing the affairs of the copra plantation, she struck Parma as being as clear-headed and logical as any man, and if she had had any doubts about her ability to talk business on her father's behalf, they had now melted away. All the same, it was more than likely there was another reason as well for her visit to the Butterfly Montane.

Yet if there *was* a love affair working up between Pierce and Glenda it was, in Parma's book, a pretty cool and unromantic one. She could not imagine the planter falling helplessly in love. He had probably burned out that side of his nature during his entanglement with Rowena Arnold. Hadn't Helen said he had been 'insanely in love' then? Now he was hard and cynical and quite invulnerable. And Parma did her best to avoid him.

One evening she encountered him when she was in the garden, picking a few small blooms to put in her room.

'Your Didirman's attentive all of a sudden,' he said. The red light of sundown glowed on his face so that he looked overwhelmingly dramatic and exciting. Absently he reached out and took one of the white gardenias she had picked and sniffed it appreciatively. Her eyes met his and she knew he was laughing at her, implying that Alec came because of Glenda Loveday.

'Yes, I'm lucky he manages to get away now and again,' she said, hanging on to her composure and pretending not to catch his implication. 'I think it's important we see as much of each other as we can.'

'Indeed?' His look sharpened, narrowed. 'You're still seriously considering him, then?'

'What do you think?' Parma's fine eyebrows went up, but she didn't directly answer his question. He had no right to ask it, and also it was not a question she had answered satisfactorily for herself just yet. She held out her hand. 'Give me back my flower, please, before you tear it to pieces.'

'Do you really think I'd tear such a fragile thing apart?'

'I'm sure you would,' she said, colouring faintly, and seeing his lip curl.

'Here—take it, then.' She did so, and put it meticulously with the small bunch in her other hand. 'I'm disappointed. I thought a girl as romantic as you would put that particular flower aside and wear it next her heart or some such nonsense.'

What colossal conceit! Or was he joking?

'Why? Because the great planter has touched it? I'm afraid that doesn't raise *my* temperature. I leave all the adulation to Sophie Gide and Glenda Loveday.' Her dark eyes sparkled as she stared steadily at him, though her heart was hammering.

'You do? Now there's an invitation if I ever heard one!' There was a laugh on his lips and his hand reached out for her wrist so that her grip on the flowers was weakened and they fell to the grass. He swung her roughly towards him. 'I'd like to have a long, long talk with you one of these days, Miss Parma Drew, to find out exactly what makes you tick. There are times when you use the tactics of a practised seductress, yet if you're touched you react like a girl from a convent school.'

'That's only if *you* touch me,' she flashed, but there was fire in her cheeks and her blood raced. It was useless to try to escape his grip, and now, without his being even aware of it, he was trampling carelessly on her flowers.

'Why do you stay on here? Why don't you get out before you do any real damage? You know you'll never marry that Didirman. You'd be crazy if you did. We're tough out here—*your* heart is ready to break over a few trampled flowers.' He was pulling her closer now, his arm as hard and inflexible as steel, and she resisted as though her life depended on it.

'At least I have a heart,' she breathed. 'That's something *you* don't seem to know about—but Alec does.' Her wrist was hurting and her pulses were beating madly, and she hardly knew what she was saying.

He let her go suddenly and she almost fell, then crouching, began blindly to gather up her crushed flowers.

He pushed them aside contemptuously with his foot. 'They're finished. Nothing will revive them.'

'You—you killed them—and yet you talk of not tearing fragile things apart——' She stared up at him, her eyes wide.

'The flowers are nothing. But there are a few other things I'd like to kill—a few crazy notions of yours, Parma Drew!'

He turned savagely on his heel and left her crouching on the ground like a native woman. Her tears fell soundlessly on the crushed flowers whose sweet scent drifted sickeningly upwards...

The following Sunday Parma at last went to Varmari.

She and Alec had been to the river pool in the morning, but for once the other two failed to join them. It was a dull day, warm, oppressive, the clouds that covered the sky hanging low and brooding. The pool had none of its usual sparkle, the tangle jungle of trees looked dark and uninviting and the river's song was moody. Parma, thinking of the picnic basket they had brought, felt despondent. Alec was edgy today, his charm submerged, and she suspected he was thinking of Glenda whose company he pretty obviously found more stimulating than her own.

So it was Parma who presently said, 'Let's take our *kai* back to the bungalow, Alec. I don't really think it's the right day for the river, do you? I don't wonder the others didn't come.'

He gave a faint uncaring shrug. 'If that's the way

you want it. Though I thought I was being perfectly unobjectionable this morning. I've left you well alone, haven't I?'

Parma flushed. He sounded as if he wanted to pick a quarrel with her, and it did not seem to occur to him that he had been leaving her 'well alone' ever since Glenda Loveday had come to the Butterfly Montane. She said quietly, 'Is that how you feel about me, Alec?'

'That you want me to leave you alone?' He was sitting on a boulder. He had pulled his shirt on over his swimming shorts and was looking darkly into the water while Parma stood combing the tangles from her long wet hair. 'You haven't left me in much doubt about that, have you? Any time I want to kiss you you wriggle out of my arms as though I intended to seduce you.'

There was too much truth in that for her to deny it, and so she said nothing.

'You are a very seductive girl, you know,' said Alec after a moment. 'That hit me right in the eyes the first time we met—at the school. But since you've been here, I've been beginning to think that appearances can be deceptive. Or maybe there's someone else around whom you find more exciting.' He sprang up suddenly and said briskly, 'Right, then. Let's get back to the bungalow. Maybe it's what we both want.'

Parma, whose mouth had opened on a soundless exclamation a couple of times while he was speaking, picked up her dress and sandals and rather thoughtfully made for the bamboo clump where she always changed. It had amazed her that Alec should call her seductive. It was one of the last epithets she would ever have thought of applying to herself. And that other thing he had said—suggested—— Her hands were unsteady as she pulled the zipper that closed the back of her yellow cotton. 'Maybe there's someone else around whom you find more exciting.' He could mean only one person, of course: Pierce Adams. And Pierce was one man she could barely tolerate.

She fastened the straps of her sandals, stood up, and shook her dark hair back, feeling its cold damp strands against her neck and upper arms. Her mind had gone for the moment conveniently blank, she was aware of nothing but physical sensations. Yet she knew that Alec had started a train of thought that she would have, some time, to follow. No matter where it led. *She* had thought it was for Alec's sake she had suggested returning to the bungalow. Was it for herself too—and for a reason other than that this way she wouldn't have to face a whole afternoon alone with him?

Neither of them had much to say as they ate a rather late lunch on the Barlows' verandah. David and Helen had gone out and Parma was not going to suggest, now, that they go and see if the others were around. Neither, apparently, was Alec. Parma, going inside to make the inevitable pot of coffee, reflected that they might just as well have stayed down at the river.

When she came back, Pierce and Glenda were there: Glenda draped gracefully on a bamboo lounge, wearing flowered cotton trousers and matching sleeveless top, Pierce leaning idly against one of the verandah posts. Parma's heart seemed to turn over at the sight of him—big, sun-tanned, hard-looking, his blue-green eyes inscrutable as he turned his head to say hello.

'Don't offer us a thing, Parma,' said Glenda, leaning back in the lounger. 'We're both very well fed, aren't we, Pierce?'

'We are indeed,' he agreed.

Parma put the tray down on a table and handed a cup to Alec with a hand that shook. She knew he was watching Glenda, though his eyes were half closed. She went to stand beside Pierce at the verandah rail, but not too close, where she couldn't see him unless she turned his way.

'Glenda's keen to meet the anthropologist at Varmari,' Pierce said, as though continuing a conversation that had been interrupted. 'What about it, Alec? When's a good time?'

'He'll be gone in a day or two,' said Alec. 'He's clearing up his notes now.'

'Hmm. Then today may be our last chance.' He glanced at his watch. 'We'd have to go almost right away if we're not to be too late home. I don't suppose we can expect you to rustle up anything for us for an evening meal?'

'No,' agreed Alec. 'Not at such short notice. Sorry about that, Glenda.'

'Don't think about it, Alec. I know how it is.'

Pierce said, 'Parma——' and she turned her head instantly, instinctively, and found his eyes challenging her. Want to come?' He didn't even wait for her to answer that, but told the others, 'When I first met Parma, do you know what she asked me?—"Would you please tell me how to get to Varmari?"'

Parma bit her lip and turned away blindly. He was intent on making a fool of her.

'Well, we'll show you the way to Varmari today,' said Glenda kindly. 'I've never actually been there, but I have a fair idea of what to expect of these tiny government stations. I guess it's a bit rough and primitive, Alec?'

'You could say that. But one gets used to it.'

Parma went in Alec's jeep, and the other two followed in the Land-Rover. Parma had never been so far up into the mountains before. As they negotiated the rough narrow dirt road at some speed, she wondered how they would manage to get back in the dark. She would have to come back with Pierce, of course. But he probably knew these roads even better than Alec. He had lived here longer.

All around was jungle now, frightening and dark under the lowering sky. Now and again they passed a native village built around a clearing on some ridge—

a position of advantage in case of attack! Somewhere in the vicinity were the inevitable subsistence gardens, where the women toiled day after day, digging and weeding, and gathering food for the families' needs. Alec spoke only occasionally, but he was intent on the road. They were driving through rain now, and they passed a native walking along the roadside holding up a big black umbrella. He wore a headdress of possum fur and short feathers, and there was a cassowary quill through his nose. Otherwise he wore nothing but a long frontal apron of cords that reached almost to the ground, and a bunch of leaves at the back. In front of him, nose to the ground, trotted a fat black pig, on a lead that was tied to one of its front legs.

Alec didn't comment. To him it was probably an everyday sight and he hardly noticed it. But Parma was filled with a sense of amusement and astonishment. Somehow a sight like that made her wonder about everything in her life that she took so much for granted—food and clothing and convention and transport, the western way of life, the complications of civilised living. She wished with all her heart that Alec would talk to her—would wonder with her. Instead, he stared stolidly ahead, and the jungle-covered mountains about him could have been non-existent. She wondered what he thought about, apart from keeping the jeep on the road. In his way, he was as mysterious to her as that primitive man with the umbrella and his precious pig.

They passed a small mission station with a little square bush building that Alec said was a school, and not very long afterwards they reached Varmari—a tiny air-strip, which Parma guessed would be accessible only in good weather, and then only by helicopter or a very small plane, and a few scattered dismal-looking buildings. Privately, Parma was shocked. Somehow she had imagined Varmari Station as neat and clean and efficient-looking. But primitive was the word ... Alec's house was of rough timber with walls woven from palm leaves and a thick thatched roof of kunai grass. It looked to consist of two rooms and a ramshackle verandah. Behind it was a native hut, where the *hausboi* lived.

A dog barked as they pulled up and Alec shouted '*Raus!*' Parma sat where she was while he climbed out. He seemed totally unconscious of the fact that Varmari might be something of a shock to her.

'Wait a bit, and I'll see if Doug's around,' he told her, and strode off in the direction of a small bush house perched on the edge of a gully behind a more respectable building that would be, she thought, the post office—and the Medical Officer's house. A few native children, dusty and almost naked, came to stare from the bush. Parma could hear—weirdly—someone playing the mouth organ. It was the anthropologist, she decided, because the sound stopped suddenly when Alec reached the guest house.

Rain was falling, grey and fine and misty. Though it was not cold, Parma sat shivering in the jeep until Pierce's Land-Rover arrived.

Pierce and Glenda got out immediately and came across to the jeep.

Parma said, 'Alec's gone to find the anthropologist.'

'Marvellous,' said Glenda. She was looking around her keenly, quite unperturbed. 'So this is where Alec hangs out! What a view down the valley!' She didn't seem to mind the rain on her face and hair, and Pierce stood, arms folded, smiling at Parma. Though it was not really her idea of a smile. There seemed to be very little friendliness about it.

She said with an attempt at casualness, 'It's beautiful, isn't it?' and saw his mouth twist sardonically.

Alec came back in a moment, walking quickly through the rain.

'Doug says to come over. He has some beer and biscuits, and he's not averse to female company.' Reluctantly, Parma clambered out of the jeep. She didn't really fancy being cooped up in a tiny bush house while people talked over her head.

'I can't imagine five of us crammed into that steamy hut,' Pierce said surprisingly. 'Parma and I will leave it to you two while we take a walk around. Do you have any rain capes, Alec?'

'I'll organise a search,' said Alec. He looked at Parma unsmilingly. 'That okay with you? Or would you rather I got the *hausboi* to make you some tea, and you could sit on my verandah?' His eyes watched her sharply and she felt discomfited, remembering what he had said.

'She can drink tea anywhere,' said Pierce before she had managed a reply. 'Besides, she wants to see Varmari.' There was a glitter in his eyes, and the two men looked at each other with dislike—there was no mistaking it.

'I'll be all right, Alec,' said Parma. Glenda, who was not interested in anyone else's plans, was heading for the guest house, and after a second Alec said, 'You'll find something to keep you dry in my house. Just give a yell for Martin.' He turned and followed Glenda.

It was Pierce who gave a yell for Martin, and the *hausboi* appeared immediately.

'*Mipela laik saket bilong rein*,' Pierce told him, and he came back in a moment with capes made of beaten bark—soft and almost as pliant as vellum, though not so clean! Parma forgot the impersonal and comfortless look of Alec's house, and couldn't help smiling as she put the *sekit bilong rein* over her head and set out with Pierce for a tour of Varmari. She would show him that nothing could daunt her! She gave only a fleeting thought to those other two in the guest house sharing beer and biscuits with an anthropologist called Doug. Glenda, who looked so sophisticated and poised and beautiful, would be at home anywhere—particularly if there were a couple of admiring men around——

She followed Pierce along the narrow track, and then he took a path that led up a steep hill through thick jungle. Soon they reached a cleared area, and there, clinging to the hillside, were the subsistence gardens, neatly laid out in terraces, with long ditches dug for drainage. A stout fence of pointed casuarina sticks surrounded the gardens, and by the fence was a heavy vine rope, reaching from the track right to the highest garden. It would help to haul yourself up, Parma realised, and she pitied the women whose lives consisted in trudging up here every day to work, rain or shine, bringing their little children with them, and at the end of the day carrying back heavy loads of sweet potato and other vegetables, and probably firewood too, on their backs.

She stood panting a little, lips parted, brows creased, and Pierce looked down at her.

'Well? What's troubling you now?'

'I—I was thinking of the women,' she said.

'It's their way of life,' he said gently. Then—'I wish you could see yourself in that rain cloak! And the tip of that little straight nose of yours is wet. Are you sure you want to go on?'

Long ago, she remembered, he had said she was made of sugar and spice—that she would melt in the rain. She wondered if he remembered that now as she did. But she would not melt in the rain—and he was going to be made to realise it.

'Of course I'm sure. Now that I'm here——'

He looked down at her with wickedly smiling eyes. 'You're not afraid of me?'

'Why should I be?'

He said nothing at all for a second, but continued to look at her, still faintly smiling. 'You really don't know, do you?' he said lightly. *'Maski.'* He held out his hand. 'Come and I'll show you a bridge.'

Her feet slipped as she followed him down through the jungle again, and his hand gripped hers more

131

tightly. The ground was wet and treacherous, raindrops dripped from her cloak. Somewhere near by a bird gave its harsh ugly cry. Pierce said, 'That's the Bird of Paradise. Shows you can't have everything, doesn't it?'

'Yes.' She knew very well that one could not have everything. Probably there was something that even Glenda Loveday wanted and could not have ...

The bridge he wanted to show her hung over a deep and narrow gully where a brown river swung turbulently. It was a native bridge made of long thin saplings, supported by two thick swinging vines. The footway was no more than four inches wide, and every few feet, for support and strength, more vines had been tied around the saplings and fastened to the others, which formed the only handrail.

'Want to cross?' Pierce asked. His eyes glinted and there were drops of moisture on the points of his straight dark lashes. His easy kindness of a while ago had vanished, and now he looked tauntingly diabolical. He didn't think she would dare step on to that narrow bridge.

She pushed back a strand of dark hair that had fallen forward from under her bark rain cape. 'Of course I want to go across. That's what bridges are for, isn't it?'

He raised his eyebrows. 'Exactly. That's a very wise statement. Will you go first, or shall I?'

'I'll go first,' said Parma. She had taken no more than three steps when the bridge began to sway giddily, and her knuckles whitened as she clutched hard at the thick wiry vines to steady herself. From behind her, Pierce asked lightly, 'Still want to go across? It will sway more than this, you know.'

Parma didn't answer him. She was moving ahead again, thankful that he could not see the tension in her face. Now she could feel him close behind her and the knowledge of his nearness steadied and strengthened her. Of course it must be safe enough. It was just a little unnerving at first, that was all. And the river was such a long way down. Many people must walk across this bridge. Alec probably used it almost daily. She was becoming accustomed to the swinging and swaying, but she kept her eyes away from the gully and the rushing river below. She had no head for heights. She just kept telling herself, 'Another few steps and you'll be safe on the other side.'

'Well, you did it,' said Pierce as at last they stood at the other side.

'Yes.' She breathed quickly and unevenly, and looked back across the bridge that was still swinging.

'How long would a bridge like that last, Pierce?'

'Do you really want to know?' Her question seemed to surprise him. 'Two or three years, maybe. There are many of them around these hills. The natives put them across. Occasionally you may find one that's been cut down in the course of tribal battle—but tribal wars are becoming more and more a thing of the past. This particular bridge is likely to stay until someone— maybe your Didirman—decides it's no longer safe, but I don't think that will be for a while yet. You're very safe, really. Think you can make it back to the other side? We'd better not stay away too long.'

'Of course I can make it.' But she hesitated. Somehow, she was reluctant to go back to the others just yet. She was happy wandering round here—even with Pierce Adams!

This time she was not nearly so nervous, and she found she had rapidly acquired the knack of balancing herself as the footway swung from side to side. As they walked on together, she asked him, 'How do people get around here, Pierce? There don't seem to be many roads.'

'I thought Alec would have told you all about that. No, there aren't many roads. A jeep or a motorcycle is pretty handy, but there's still a lot of walking to do.

The wilderness and inaccessibility of these mountains is one of our biggest problems in the Highlands.'

Parma walked beside him, trying to match her step to his, and listening intently, eager to learn more about this country.

'Go on,' she prompted when he paused.

'Most of the roads have been made by the natives, by sheer hard physical work. There's no machinery up here, no easy way. But they need their roads if they're to share in the benefits of civilisation, and if they're to sell their cash crops. The Butterfly Montane buys coffee beans from some of the small native groves even as far out as this. The indigenes carry their bags of stuff down to the roadside on the days they know one of us—David or myself—will be driving out.'

The rain had thickened and they stopped in the shelter of a heavily foliaged tree. Parma felt happy because it delayed their return to the station and she was enjoying everything just now—even the rain and Pierce Adams' company! She looked up at him as he was speaking and it occurred to her that she knew his face pretty well by heart now—those gold-flecked eyes with their dark masculine lashes, that firm chin, those lips that were so often curled in mockery or derision. Today there was a softness in his expression as he talked to her so patiently. It reminded her of the gentleness she had so often observed in him when she saw him playing with little Elisabet. And she remembered the night at the Sports Club when he had promised her that Alec would come back to her. He was, she supposed, in many ways a wise and kindly man. His *hausboi* was devoted to him, she had never heard Helen or David say a word against him, he was liked and respected by his labour force. The harshness and mockery that she knew were only for her. And that was because of an unfortunate parallel he drew between herself and a girl called Rowena Arnold. Helen had told her once, 'Knowing his story, you will be able to understand him better.' Perhaps she did, but it didn't make it much easier to put up with the role of scapegoat.

Now he moved to find cigarettes, pushing his rain cape back. When he had finished with shielding the flame of his lighter, he said more briskly, 'Well, you must have got at least some idea today of how Alec lives. Isn't that so? The size and inaccessibility of the station will have told you a lot. Next to no creature comforts, supplies in only every month or so, electricity available only a few hours each day. No shops or bright lights or parties. Not much variety in anything. Most girls would find it more than a little dispiriting. I think even you must agree that to stand up to these conditions one's love should be based on something rather more solid than romantic dreams.' His eyes were bright and watchful now, and he was leaning back against the tree trunk in what she had observed to be one of his favourite attitudes.

Parma thought wryly, 'So this is why we came to Varmari. It wasn't just to give Glenda an opportunity to talk to the anthropologist. It was to teach me a lesson—and to speed me on my way. To show me the tough face of the land where I don't belong.' She made a small grimace.

'Is this a lecture for my moral good?'

'You could say that,' he said laconically. 'Or that it's for the moral good of us all ... You did think it romantic, didn't you, to have Alec Rivers fall in love with you back in Sydney? But isn't it time now to stop fooling yourself? You've had a nice long game of make-believe, and I'm sure you've enjoyed yourself mightily. But after all, it *is* just a game, isn't it? All this running around in native rain cloaks and swinging about on dangerous-looking bridges. Making generous gestures to little native children. Even frightening yourself when your car broke down—though that was going a bit too far, wasn't it?'

He paused and Parma stared at him speechlessly. He certainly knew how to hurt—and he had hurt her bitterly. The pleasure she had found in the gift to Elisabet—her happiness today with *him*—her little victory over the bridge—they lay in fragments around her. He blew smoke into the rain and didn't look her way, or he might have seen her stricken face.

'You're not even remotely interested in settling down here with us, Parma. I think you intended right from the start that when you'd had enough you'd pack up your bags and say you were sorry—that you'd tried—but now you were faced with the sad and unalterable facts that there was some deep, crying need within you that couldn't be satisfied by what this country has to offer.'

He could not have sounded more cynical. He was quoting, of course. That was what Rowena Arnold had told *him* when she packed her bags and left. Parma felt more than a little angry. She had nothing in common with Rowena Arnold.

'You know all about me, don't you?' she said, her colour rising. 'I just don't need to say a thing.'

'Not to me you don't. Girls like you are bad medicine for any man here who values his self-respect and integrity.'

That didn't strike home. No one could say she was 'bad medicine' for Alec—Alec simply had never intended asking her to share his life. She knew that now, and she thought the planter had known it for a long time.

'I think perhaps it would be better if you left me alone,' she said huskily. 'You didn't *have* to bring me out here, you know. You didn't *have* to take me walking in the rain. I could have done without my—my swing on the bridge.' Tears were not far from her eyes but she refused to admit them, and faced him unblinkingly, her small chin up.

'I'll leave you alone the day you pack your stuff and

go home,' he said.

'And you won't be satisfied until that happens,' thought Parma. It was a shattering, devastating thought and she recoiled from it as from a physical blow. Shaken, she looked up into his eyes, greenish gold on this day of rain and cloud. All her feeling of anger and animosity had gone. Those eyes baffled her. She simply didn't know what she read there as they gazed steadily back, seeming to penetrate to her innermost being, to the very stricken heart of her. Questioning, searching, probing. Pierce's eyes ... Suddenly her lashes came down as with a shock of fear she realised what might be read in her own.

She turned away blindly, head down, and began to walk into the rain. Her heart was thudding and a voice within her was crying out so loudly that she had to listen, 'I love him—I love him' ... It was for *him* she had wanted to prove her toughness, her adaptability. It was for *him* she had wanted to learn this savage land. He was the one man for whom she would go anywhere —dare anything.

She walked faster as though to escape from the truth she had discovered, her feet slipping on dead leaves, the bark cape falling back so that the rain blew against her face and hair and her thin cotton dress ...

Back at the station, Alec had Martin make coffee and they drank it sitting on the verandah of his house while rain dripped from the thatched roof. The anthropologist had declined to join them as he wanted to get his notes written up, but Glenda appeared stimulated by her hour or so of talk and Parma, sitting a little apart and avoiding looking in Pierce's direction, wondered vaguely if Doug too had fallen under her spell.

She sat in the back of the Land-Rover going home. It was growing dark and the fine misty rain continued. Glenda talked animatedly and intelligently about the anthropologist and his work, and Pierce put in an occasional comment or two. He even once or twice politely asked Parma her opinion—which she was sure he could hardly value! She caught herself committing to memory the back of his head—the way the dark gold hair grew on his neck, the easy but proud set of his broad shoulders—and now and again she looked quickly in the rear vision mirror where, until it grew too dark, she could see the upper half of his face reflected. Insane self-torture! For not even once did she catch his eye.

Glenda's brown hair was curly with the damp, and little loose tendrils made ringlets on the back of her neck. They made a very handsome couple, thought Parma with a twist in her heart. He would never have to wonder if *Glenda* would suddenly pack up and go.

Her thoughts went only once to Alec, and then it was to reflect that he had suspected what was happening to her before it had even vaguely occurred to Parma. He had told her long ago, 'I don't think Pierce Adams would find you particularly to his liking.' Had he been warning her even then? Now, unaware, she had followed to its end the train of thought he had started in her mind this morning, and it had led her to this bitter cul-de-sac where there was no going on. But for her there was no turning back, either. And so the planter was right. It was time for her to go ...

CHAPTER NINE

AND yet she made no move to go. Too easily she allowed herself to be persuaded when Helen protested, 'But we *love* having you, Parma. The girls won't be home these holidays, and besides, I'm depending on you to help me get *Tok Kuskus* finished. You can't possibly go yet.'

And so Parma was consoled and persuaded that she did right to stay. Just a little longer . . .

When the Land-Rover was not there and she knew Glenda and Pierce were away from the bungalow, she sometimes walked alone through the garden or under the coffee trees on the plantation. And whenever she heard the sound of the gong, although she knew it was only *belo*, something in her imaginative nature translated it into magic. Games—romance! How Pierce Adams would deride her! She had not seen him since the visit to Varmari and Alec did not come to the plantation that week as he had to be away from the station.

One afternoon when she knew Pierce was away, she went over to see Pawpaw and little Elisabet, and played with the child, teaching her a few English words and some little rhymes while her mother did the washing. She was taken by surprise when Glenda appeared and asked if she would like to join her for coffee.

Glenda seemed very much at home in the planter's house, and to Parma it was obvious that it would not be long before she was permanently installed there.

They had their coffee on the verandah, and when Glenda went inside for the cream which she liked and that Unkapenna simply refused point blank to provide, as she put it, she came back with a sheet of paper.

A sheet that had been torn and mended.

Parma felt the colour leave her cheeks when she saw it.

'Look what I found on Pierce's desk this morning.' Glenda held it out for Parma to see. So he had not destroyed it, and he had not given it to Elisabet. For of course it was the drawing of the child chasing the butterfly—Parma in her futile quest for love. It was like a knife twisting in her heart to see that drawing, and now the symbolism seemed more poignant than ever. She almost exclaimed, 'It's my drawing!' But an acute sensitivity held her back.

'It's sweet, isn't it?' said Glenda. 'I wonder why he keeps it? Could it possibly be for some sentimental reason? He's a complex character, our Pierce, isn't he? I never have the faintest idea what's going on behind that masterful front of his. Did you ever see anything like this? It's charming—but it's the essence of corny romanticism. It must have some sort of personal significance for him that he doesn't throw it out.'

Parma murmured vaguely. Glenda was quite wrong about that drawing, she knew. Pierce Adams had simply forgotten about it, that was all.

Pierce came back to the bungalow before Parma had gone, and she felt the colour rush to her face then ebb away, leaving her weak and shaken, as he came along the verandah to join them. Her reply to his greeting was scarcely audible, but through her lashes she watched him settle in a bamboo chair, his long legs stretched out comfortably before him, as he reached for cigarettes. He looked tired, she thought, the usually firm line of his mouth was relaxed and a little sad. He paid no particular attention to her, and for that she was glad, being quite content to sit and look covertly at him.

He had been to the Gides' plantation, she soon discovered, as he told Glenda in answer to her questions that things were as bad as they could be.

'They've no more than a skeleton work-force now, and I can't make out whether it's because Arthur simply can't afford the wages or because the men refuse to work for him. He's so cagey these days one can't get much out of him.'

'I don't know why you bother about those two, Pierce,' Glenda said lazily. She was looking alluring in one of her exclusive bordered cottons. 'I've never met a more hopelessly inefficient and pig-headed pair. Frankly, they reduce me to screaming point, particularly that droopy Sophie. Which is why I simply refuse to go there again ... Why don't you make an offer for the estate—anonymously if you like—and buy them out? That would be my advice. You can afford it, and honestly, you'd be doing them both a service.'

Pierce closed his eyes tiredly. 'I'm not at all sure that I would. Arthur has a battle to fight—psychologically as well as materially. He's got to prove something to himself. Maybe, somehow, he'll make it. I don't know. I admit that in spite of everything I have a lot of respect for Arthur. As for Sophie, you're too hard on her, Glenda. She's very young.'

'I'm beginning to suspect there's a strong streak of sentimentality in your make-up, Pierce,' said Glenda, sending Parma a sudden veiled smile. Parma's heart began to pound, and it was all she could do to prevent herself from jumping up and running away. But to her relief, Glenda said nothing more, and the moment was over. If she had mentioned that drawing in Pierce's presence, she thought she would have died of humiliation. She much preferred that he should go on ignoring her—talking as though she were not there. That way, at least she could enjoy the sight of him— which might be completely futile but still gave her an acute pleasure. And reminded her, when she stopped to think about it, of what he had told her about the palm leaf basket, long ago. Soon enough, she would be left with not even a handful of dust ...

'I'm not sentimental,' said Pierce. 'Far from it. I finished with that sort of thing long ago. I admire Arthur because he's trying to perform an almost super-human task. And it worries me that he's overworking himself to an almost criminal extent.'

Glenda opened her beautiful hazel eyes wide. 'He's overworking that dotty little sister of his too, isn't he? *She*'ll have a breakdown if she doesn't watch out. There's no more flesh on her bones than there is on Parma's here and yet she gets out among the trees be-side her admirable brother and tries to do a man's work. Which in my view shows a sad lack of intelli-gence whether she's young or not. If I were in her shoes, I'd soon face Arthur with a few facts.'

Pierce turned his head and looked at Parma through half shut gold-flecked eyes. She, caught out staring, bit her lip fiercely. 'What do you think, Parma? Do you think a woman should work along with a man to help him attain his ends regardless of her own desires?'

Parma's gaze was still caught in his. She was remem-bering how he had lectured her at Varmari, how he had told her she had never had any intention of set-tling down in New Guinea. Now he spoke to her coolly, detachedly, as if none of that had ever been. He even asked her opinion! Perhaps he wanted to know what effect his lecturing had had.

'I—I would do whatever he wanted,' she stammered.

Glenda looked at her sharply. 'Why?'

'Because—because what a man does with his life is important.'

'And what a woman does with hers is not?' Glenda laughed pityingly. 'You funny child! I don't believe you've ever heard of Women's Lib.'

'Parma believes in love,' drawled Pierce. He was not looking at her now, but into the garden where butter-flies hovered over the bright flowers. 'Romantic love. Unfortunately, she's not very adept at handling facts. But she and I are in agreement on one point. A man's work—his place in life—are important to him. If a woman doesn't respect them, then she doesn't belong with him.'

'But as Sophie is Arthur's sister, and not his wife,' said Glenda, sitting forward and smiling up at Pierce, 'none of what we are saying is really relevant, is it? If Sophie was being victimised by a *husband*, I should find it pathetic but excusable. As she is being victimised by her brother, I find it simply—pathetic. A woman can be intelligent in her choice of a husband, and I for one am not so stupid as to fall in love with an unsuitable man.'

'And *I* am not so stupid as to be unable—or unwilling—to adapt myself to the needs of the man I fall in love with,' said Parma in a flash. Her words surprised even herself, and she stood up quickly to cover her confusion. Pierce, who must think she was referring to Alec, was looking at her thoughtfully, while Glenda looked more than slightly displeased. 'It's time I was going,' she told them huskily. 'Thank you for the coffee, Glenda.'

'Think nothing of it.' Glenda was cool now. 'Come again.'

Come again—to the bungalow that would soon belong to Glenda as well as to Pierce ... Parma walked quickly away from them, through Pierce's tangled, sweet smelling tropical garden. A Blue Mountain butterfly hovered over a spire of yellow ginger blossom. It caused her a pang and she felt annoyed with herself. She was sentimental, romantic, all the things they despised. She wondered what they were talking about now she had gone, those two on the verandah. They would have forgotten about her already. Maybe they would be talking about love. Though it would not be *her* idea of love. She thought that Glenda was very cold-blooded about loving Pierce. He was a 'suitable' man. And after his experience with Rowena Arnold, he would think her a 'suitable' woman.

Neither of them would have to make any concessions, any sacrifices, any efforts at understanding. Their marriage would be all plain sailing. The only things that would be lacking would be the important things— warmth and excitement and wonder. Parma had thought she had found those things in Alec, but she had been wrong. Now she was crazy enough to dream she could have found them with Pierce. If only——

But thinking 'if only' got you nowhere. She should try to emulate Glenda and fall in love sensibly—with someone who would feel the same way about her. So far, she had failed lamentably. First William Cunningham, then Alec, and now Pierce Adams! Yes, Glenda's was the wise way. But she would never be able to follow it—never. Her heart was too wayward for that. It was a bleak thought.

The following day, after a restless night, and a brief unrefreshing sleep, Parma woke late. Even *belo* had not disturbed her, and when she got up the sun was already hot. She hurried out to the breakfast room to find the dishes cleared away and Helen dressed ready to go out. Beyond the verandah David, instead of being out on the plantation supervising the work, was checking the radiator of his car.

'I'm sorry, I didn't wake up. You should have called me. Are you going out?'

'David has to go into town, and I'm going with him.'

'Oh.' Parma looked at her uncertainly. Was she not to be invited?

'In fact, we're just about to leave. I was going to write a note for you. Pierce came in early to say he wants you to go to a *singsing* in one of the mountain villages this evening. It will certainly be a lot more fun than Kundalufa, so I accepted on your behalf. They'll be leaving at about four, I should imagine. Do you think you'll be able to fill in the time till then?'

'Yes, of course.' Parma's tongue touched her upper

lip. She felt more dismayed than she could say, and more than a little puzzled too. So Pierce 'wanted' her to go to a *singsing*, did he? This was something new, for him to more or less dictate what she was to do! Her wakeful meditations of the previous night had led her to the conclusion that it would be good sense to forget about Pierce Adams. And the idea of attending a *singsing* with him and Glenda was unnerving, to say the least.

Well, it was too late to go to Kundalufa with the Barlows now, but she would certainly not go to that *singsing*. She was not going to subject herself to that, no matter what Pierce 'wanted'. And no matter how her heart ached for him.

All morning she tried to become absorbed in typing Helen's stories, but continually Pierce's face came between her and the words, and she made error after error. She was a mass of jangling nerves, and afraid moreover that she would suddenly look up and find him standing in the doorway. Subconsciously, she probably wished that she would, she reflected wryly— she had reached that stage. She was more or less possessed by him.

He didn't come, and she saw no one but Pawpaw and Elisabet when she looked across to the other bungalow.

At lunchtime, she made herself a salad and found orange juice in the fridge, and when she had eaten and cleared up her dishes, she lay down on her bed and feel asleep.

When she woke, to her dismay it was nearly four. In her panic, she could think of only one thing to do, and that was to get away from the bungalow as quickly as possible. They could be here any minute now, and she was quite sure Pierce would override any objections she had to going with them. Moreover, she was too well aware of her own weakness. One look at that dark strong face, one glance from those compelling eyes with their gold-tipped lashes and all her good resolutions would dissolve away. She would go like a lamb to the slaughter and suffer anew the torture of her mad, unwanted love for him. And if Alec had suspected it before she had become aware of it herself, then Glenda or even Pierce himself might read it in her face now that she was conscious of it. And that she could not bear.

Almost without thinking, she pulled one of her cotton dresses over her head, slipped her feet into sandals, dragged a comb through her dark hair, and practically flew outside to Helen's car. The keys were always left in it, there was plenty of petrol, and with a guilty look around she started it up, swung it around, and was off down the track through the plantation—driving fast and raising a cloud of dust.

Belo sounded as she reached the roadway, and she breathed a sigh of relief. She turned towards Varmari, though she had no intention of going there, and began to drive more steadily. It was hot and sunny, but the usual clouds drifted across the pale blue sky and it was pleasant driving.

She settled down to an even pace and allowed her thoughts to wander where they would. They wandered of course to Pierce, and inevitably to Glenda with her beauty and intelligence, and her enormous self-assurance. There was a very easy comradely relationship between her and the planter, and Parma had no doubt that if they married, it would be a marriage that would work. She was conscious of the searing, burning pain of jealousy. Not for the first time, she wished she were different herself—in many ways . . .

Her musing was interrupted by the harsh cry of the Bird of Paradise from the jungle, and she thought bleakly, 'Glenda has everything. Including Pierce. Ah well, we can't all be poised and beautiful and—Territorian.' It was a bitter and unalterable fact, and one that she must learn to live with. Though so long as she remained here, she would never do that. So—of course —she must make a definite move, and go. This would have to be the last time she would ever drive along these roads. Next car trip she took would be in the direction of Kundalufa and the airstrip.

Alec did not enter her thoughts at all.

She drove doggedly on, up and up into the mountains, until she was negotiating bends and steep pinches that would have frightened her into a fit at any ordinary time. The jungle was closing in around her so thickly that she no longer seemed to be in touch with civilisation at all. She must have got on to one of the forbidden side tracks long ago. The few natives she saw she now took completely for granted as they appeared from nowhere with their bundles of vegetables and firewood and babies. They walked almost naked through the jungle, some leading pigs on leads as a European would lead a dog, and their personal adornment ranged from streaks of coloured clay to the spendour of Paradise feathers.

She didn't want to leave this land ever, she knew that now. In her heart she belonged here, and she loved it almost as she loved the planter—crazily, dementedly. But for him, she barely existed . . .

She came to her senses when suddenly the narrow track, deeply shadowed by jungle, petered out. It just did not go on and she was forced to pull up, which she did with a jerk. She wondered half dazedly where she was and whether she had temporarily taken leave of her senses. She had the feeling of being very close to the sky—to that pale blue, cloud-inhabited sky of which one was always acutely aware in the highland country. Yes, she seemed very close to the clouds, very much involved with them.

She got out of the car and for no good reason at all began to walk. She climbed stolidly on and up, pushing her way through ferns and shrubs and vines, between dark trees that grew thick and heavy and close together. She climbed on until it seemed the sun had gone and she was moving in a world of white, misty, drifting cloud.

Suddenly she stood stock still, her mouth open on a silent exclamation of awe. This was the cloud forest of the folk tales! She had thought it legendary—a fabled land as the devil-pig was a fabled creature. But it was real!—if you could call such a spectral, fantastic, eerie world real at all.

The ground was soft with layer upon layer of mosses and ferns and leaves, and she knew a sense of profound wonder. She had dreamed of wandering in it, and it had been like a fairy place, with its emerald mosses and silver mist, and bright flowers that glowed like jewels. And now here she was, right in the middle of her own dream. Hidden away from any real world, surrounded by one so floating and misty that it seemed not tangible at all. Parma wondered if she herself had any substance, any weight, and in actual fact it was almost as though she were no more than a wraith. Her feet were soundless on the spongy ground, she walked in a setting for some story of the sleeping beauty—or of the twelve dancing princesses, who descended nightly into a world that existed beyond the confines of the real one. Anything could happen here.

All about her floated a silver mist, and from trees that reached up to an invisible sky, soft growing tendrils reached down—ribbon ferns, ferns like fine green glinting thread, ferns like feathers—green and gold and russet. Orchids, exotic and strange and beautiful, clung to moss-wreathed branches, and there was water everywhere. Tiny crystal streamlets tumbled at her feet, cascading in miniature waterfalls between moss grown boulders.

Somewhere a frog began to croak, high-pitched and soft at first, then louder and more insistent—a thin metallic sound, pulsing with the rhythm of a fairy drum. And behind it, so faint that she must be imagining it, was the beat of the kundu.

Parma swung the fine dark hair back from her face and stood listening. Beyond the drip- drip of moisture on the spongy ground she could hear another sound—the hush-hush-hush of feet running between the trees. The kundu drums sounded louder—though muffled, they were real. And now through the mist figures appeared—the shadows of prancing, dancing, flying natives, moving in swift single file. Tall feathery head-dresses glowed dimly red and gold, bows and arrows made dark pencil lines against the fleeting mist. Parma held her breath. The drip-drip of moisture from tree and fern, the pad-pad-pad of running feet, the heart-throb pulse of the kundu drums. An occasional muffled shout that was like a cry of life and joy from a world that was a shadow world . . .

When at last the fantastic figures had vanished, she let out her breath slowly. That this should be happening to her, Parma Drew, who had once broken her heart over a clerk called William Cunningham!

Suddenly she stiffened. Someone else had appeared out of the drifting mist. The tall dark shadow came nearer—nearer—assumed form and features.

It was Pierce Adams.

CHAPTER TEN

SHE stared at him as though he could not be real, and her heart began a steady drumming as he drew near. One part of her wanted to run away, and yet there was nothing in the world that she wanted more than to be with him. But what about the *singsing*? And what of Glenda Loveday? She glanced beyond him, certain that Glenda must be there too, but the drifting mist closed in and there was no one.

'Is there a ghost behind me?' He sounded amused and his green-gold eyes smiled at her as he came soundlessly over the mossy ground.

Parma shook her head. She couldn't look away from him, but she was still in a dream—completely caught up in a world of fantasy. Pierce's presence here seemed to prove it.

'How—how did you find me?' He was close to her now and she looked up into that dark, powerful face capped by mist-wet dark gold hair.

'How do you think I found you? Through sheer instinct, Parma Drew.'

She was puzzled by some unfamiliar note in his voice, some unfamiliar expression in his eyes. 'But how could that be?'

'Do you want facts? I didn't know you dealt in them ... Well then—I saw you careering off along the road in Helen's car. As I was under the impression that you and I had an assignation, I lost no more time than necessary in trailing you. Since that entailed first getting back to the bungalow and changing, I feel I did rather well, don't you? So surely I'm justified in claiming it was instinct that led me to you ... And now'— his hand, warm and hard and oddly familiar, reached out and took hold of her cold one—'now you're coming with me to that *singsing*. It's a celebration of the birth of an old *luluai*'s first grandson, and I've been given a special invitation. So I don't want to show bad manners by being late.'

She thought, as she went with him only half reluctantly, that Glenda would be waiting in the Land-Rover somewhere down through the trees. But just now she was deeply conscious of the touch of his hand on hers as she let him lead her through the cloud forest, over the spongy ground, between ferns and vines and flowering rhododendrons.

She said presently, her voice reasonable, 'I don't *have* to come to the *singsing*, you know.'

'No?' He glanced down at her, brows tilted, crystals glittering on his lashes.

'No. I drive myself here—I can easily drive back again.'

'I'm afraid you can't do that, Parma Drew, because I shan't allow it. I'm a great deal stronger than you are, and I'll use brute force if necessary.' Once, he might have said such words grimly, now his words sounded lightly humorous. 'You'd possibly end up killing yourself, or doing some sort of damage to Helen's car.'

Her mouth set obstinately. He thought she could not cope! 'I assure you I'd do no such thing——'

'Now don't try to fight me, Parma. You've got no choice, so try to put a cheerful face on it.' His voice had sharpened slightly. 'Just for a while see if you can forget your Didirman. He's not worth one hair of your head, in any case, and you'd never adjust to him in a lifetime—though you've convinced me that you're mad enough to try.'

For a moment she could not think what he was talking about, and then she recalled what she had said the day before. She had said she could adapt to the needs of the man she loved—and of course, he had thought she referred to Alec.

'So,' said Pierce, 'no long faces. This is a happy occa-

151

sion and you'd better make up your mind to enjoy yourself.'

Could she enjoy herself? Just to have her hand in his was heaven, but once they joined Glenda, that would be the end of that. She decided weakly to put off her decision for a few minutes more. For a little while at least, she could pretend that Pierce Adams was all hers...

As they came lower down the mountain the mists thinned and vanished and Parma was astonished to find that it was almost dark. Now when she thought of Helen's car she was filled with guilt. She would never find her way back along that narrow tortuous road in the dark. She had been completely crazy—completely irresponsible—to come all this way.

'You see?' Pierce said. 'You must do as I say this time, mustn't you?' He sounded vaguely kind, but she knew exactly what he must be thinking. This was a tough country, and to be able to cope you had to be tough yourself. Glenda would have managed, Glenda had it all. But Parma Drew was far from tough. She shivered a little and released her hand from his.

'The Rover's only a few yards away. I'll arrange for Helen's car to be picked up tomorrow. She'll understand. She wouldn't thank me if I allowed you to take any more risks.'

Parma gave in. There was nothing else to do. And as they walked on towards the Land-Rover, she steeled herself to face Glenda Loveday—and to take a back seat in every sense of the word.

But the Land-Rover, when they reached it, was empty.

'Where's—Glenda?' she asked, her voice husky.

'Glenda?' He sounded surprised. 'Good lord, I wouldn't dream of bringing Glenda to a *singing*. It's not at all her idea of entertainment. Besides——' He broke off to help Parma into the front seat, and by the time he had climbed in beside her he had apparently forgotten he had not finished what he was saying.

Parma felt she must be back in her dream again. An evening alone with Pierce! Alone in one sense of the word, for in actual fact she knew they would be in the midst of a crowd of perhaps hundreds. It would be a memory for her to treasure always, something to take away with her when she let the Territory in a few days' time. She sat huddled beside him, shivering in her cotton dress, though it was more with excitement than with cold.

When they reached the *singsing* ground it was completely dark, but flames leaping brightly from fires illuminated the feathered natives who surged down from the surrounding forests to the beat of kundu drums. They left the Land-Rover, and Pierce put his arm protectively around Parma's shoulders as they made their way through the crowd of highly excited natives who wore every kind of ornamentation possible, from gleaming gold lip pearlshell to huge brilliantly coloured headdresses, eight or nine feet tall. A heady sense of expectation rose in her strongly as the way opened before them, natives standing back, pushing each other back, to let the Europeans through. White teeth flashed in smiles of greeting, and more than one voice called jubilantly, 'Masta Adams!' Dark eyes gleamed, shell necklaces swung, grass skirts swished, and at last they reached the shelter of a long open hut with a thick grass roof. Parma, slightly shaken, sank down on a bamboo seat that had a cover of woven palm leaves thrown over it.

In the darkness of the dewy night, fire flames leapt, the kundu drums throbbed, and a group of fantastically dressed men began to dance. As they stamped and swayed and swung, their tall headdresses, red and blue, green and yellow, orange and purple, made a moving mass of scintillating colour.

It was like some dream festival as the spectacular displays of dancing continued. Parma liked best the groups whose headgear was made from fur and feathers, the muted lovely colours merging with the cream and bronze and tan of fibre and shell. Women wearing masses of black-seed necklaces, and each with a huge single *kinya* gleaming high on her breast, danced and sang a soft high-pitched song, beautiful in its way, weird and unforgettable. Pierce said it was about the *luluai*'s grandson—a song of praise and joy. Afterwards, a young girl whose dark skin gleamed with pig fat did a solo dance. She wore a grass skirt and a feather headdress, lavish with white cuscus fur.

Parma sat entranced, scarcely speaking, content to be beside Pierce and take it all in through her senses. The primitive music, the barbarous dress, the wild dances, were beyond comment—even beyond belief. But through it all she was still acutely conscious of the nearness of the planter, almost as bemused as she was. From somewhere, he had got her a covering for her shoulders, for the night air was fresh and her dress thin. It was a cloak of green woven grasses, cold against her skin when he first put it around her, but soon becoming warm and soft and caressing.

All the time, little children ran about, wild with excitement. Tiny ones slept in their mothers' arms, or in string *bilums* hung from the branches of trees. Pierce pointed out the *luluai*'s daughter-in-law who had produced the male baby—a fine young woman with close-cropped hair and a firm full figure. Her baby slept, completely naked, in his net bag where he was cushioned on layers of soft fresh green leaves.

At one end of the *singsing* ground, the feast that was to be enjoyed had been prepared. It was cooked in *mumus*—pits lined with hot stones upon which were placed banana leaves. The bundles of food—strips of pork, cobs of corn, *kaukau*, pounded bananas—were placed in the *mumu*, covered with more banana leaves, with grasses, with earth, and then steamed. Thick bamboo pipes protruded from the ground like funnels, and through them more water was poured occasionally. The food had been steaming for hours and would be tender and delectable, Pierce told Parma, as portions were brought to them on thick plates of leaves. They ate with their fingers, and Pierce's eyes gleamed smilingly at her in the firelight as he watched her enjoying the meal.

While they ate, there was more weird music from drum and mambu flute, and presently Pierce was summoned to talk to the old *luluai* who had invited him to the *singsing*. Parma's presence was requested too, and she found that the old chief, in his magnificent array of feathers and shells, had great dignity and nobility. He asked Pierce, in the little English that he had, if it was indeed true that white men had been to the moon, and Pierce told him gravely that it was so, and explained briefly and simply how the journey had been made in a great ship that climbed up into the heavens. The *luluai* listened, and Parma knew that it was beyond his comprehension—and yet here among his own people he was a man of great stature and learning. When Pierce had finished, the chief looked at Parma, long and strangely, and his eyes were black and very, very old. He sent for a tall bamboo container, and Parma was offered liquid poured from it into a small gourd.

She took the gourd in her hands and looked at Pierce, and he said softly, 'You must drink it—to the last drop,' and she did so while Pierce, and the *luluai* and a crowd of solemn-faced natives looked on. The drink was sweet and thin, but there was an astringently bitter taste behind its sweetness that took her breath away a little. The gourd was golden-yellow and patterned in black with drawings of fish and human figure and—though Parma was not quite sure of this— butterfly. Pierce's eyes were intent on hers as she finished the drink, and then the gourd was filled again from the bamboo container and this time it was passed

155

to Pierce. The ancient fathomless eyes of the *luluai* were fixed on him as he drank, and to Parma it seemed like a ceremony that she did not understand.

The dancing began again, and to Parma's complete astonishment, the *luluai* ceremoniously presented her with an armlet. It was made of woven fibre and had the blue-green carapaces of beetles laid across it. They were arranged in a pattern and looked like ancient jewels as they gleamed soft and pearly in the firelight. Bound to the armlet was a small tuft of feathers, small, iridescent, softly golden-brown.

The old chief spoke a few words in his own language as he made her the gift, and Parma heard herself answer, husky and low, 'Thank you—thank you—I shall keep it and treasure it for ever.' Her slender fingers touched the silky feathers delicately, and she looked up to meet Pierce's eyes—so different from the black, age-old eyes of the *luluai*.

'For ever?' he echoed softly. Her wide-eyed pleasure seemed to amuse him a little, for his eyes smiled into hers as he helped her fasten the band on her upper arm. 'You won't be able to take it away with you, Parma—not with its little tuft of *gras bilong kumul*. So maybe you'd better stay here with us after all. What do you think?'

She stared at him, suddenly stilled. It was the first time he had ever suggested she should stay here. Always, before, he had wanted nothing more than for her to pack up and go. She must be imagining all this— imagining that Pierce's eyes were looking at her softly, tenderly ... She put her hand to her temple. She felt dizzy, light-headed, and she smiled back at him, vaguely, warmly aware that her two hands were in his. And then he wrapped the grass cloak around her again.

'Come—you'd better sit down.' His eyes were strange and his voice reverberated softly in her ears. He put his arm about her and led her back to the bamboo seat with its cover of woven palm, and she leaned against the warmth of his shoulder as he sat by her side.

On the *singing* ground, the dancers were whirling madly, a blur of beads and shells and feathers and dark shining skin. Their feet stamped and thudded on the hard ground, and Parma could feel the vibrations from them and from the loud beat of the kundu through the whole of her responsive body. Her blood throbbed with the rhythm of the dance. She had the curious feeling that she was part of it all, that she was there in the very midst of all the colour and the noise and the uninhibited wildness and joy.

Yet Pierce's arm was still about her, and her head was against his shoulder, and his cheek—she thought—rested on her hair. She had lost all sense of time, hypnotised, almost drugged, with the never-endingness of this strange and unbelievable night.

She didn't remember going back to the Land-Rover with Pierce. But there was a long minute when they stood together in the darkness of the night, the singing and dancing at the ceremonial ground a feverish background, and Pierce's arms were locked around her and he took her mouth in a long sweet kiss of love ...

Or so it seemed to her, though later she wondered whether she had dreamed that kiss.

She must have slept all the way home, for when she woke in the morning it was strange to find she was in her own bed. She could not remember coming home at all. She lay with her hands behind her head, watching the sunlight move across the floor. She must surely have dreamed the happenings of last night. There was no feathered band on her arm—no token presented by a *luluai*.

Yet surely she had been to the cloud forest—surely Pierce had found her there and taken her to the *singsing* with him. She sat up, puzzled, and across the room on the long low dressing table shelf, she saw her shining armlet. She slid out of bed—she was in her slip, she discovered—and took it wonderingly in her hands, looking at the soft woven fibres, the glowing beetle carapaces, the tuft of Paradise feathers—*gras bilong kumul*! Pierce had said that. He had said, 'You won't be able to take that home with you. Maybe you'd better stay with us after all.'

Had he said that? Had he?

And afterwards—afterwards when the *singsing* was no more than a blur of sound—had he kissed her? Could it have been? Surely Pierce could never have kissed her in that way—deeply and sweetly, just as she longed for him to kiss her.

She stood, a small slender girl in her white slip, her dark hair floating across her shoulders, her eyes wide with questions. That drink the *luluai* had given her —had it been a love potion or a sleeping draught? She had felt so strange. And Pierce—he had drunk from the gourd too. Her fingers went to her lips and she stared at herself in the mirror. How could you tell if your lips had been kissed? Her armlet was proof that the night had not all been a dream, but there was nothing at all to tell her the truth about that kiss...

Everything seemed subtly different to Parma after that, and yet there was really no great difference in the way life proceeded. Alec came back from his round of the other valleys and on Friday night he and Parma went over to Pierce's bungalow. There, she didn't have even a moment alone with Pierce, who sat back in the lamplight letting Glenda and Alec do most of the talking. Parma caught his glance on her now and again. It was quizzical and good-humoured, but she could read no special message in it for herself. Glenda treated her coolly, and was as unobtrusively at ease with Pierce as ever—and still very much the hostess in his home. Parma could not make it out at all.

The following day, Alec arrived at the plantation

for the swim they had agreed on. Stepping from his jeep, he greeted Parma rather effusively, and in fact was just about to take the reluctant girl in his arms when Pierce came striding from his garden and interrupted the scene.

'Parma!' His voice was crisp and commanding. 'Go into the bungalow and pack a bag. I want you to come to Kunai Valley with me.'

Parma stared in astonishment, and Alec's bearded chin stuck out aggressively.

'Now hang on a bit—what's all this about? I've come over here to see Parma——'

'Have you? Then I'm afraid you'll have to make do with Glenda today, because Parma's coming with me. I've just had a call from Arthur. Sophie's not well.'

Alec's eyes narrowed. 'What do you mean, not well?'

'I'm not going into that just now. I don't see that it should interest you, in any case.' He looked at Parma, and there was a steady command in his eyes that she could not have disobeyed even had she wanted to. 'Hurry along, will you, Parma—there's a good girl. Glenda will keep Alec company.'

Parma said, 'I'm sorry, Alec. But if Sophie's sick——' She didn't wait any longer. She wasn't at all clear as to why Pierce had asked her to go with him, but as she ran into the bungalow she remembered that Glenda had said she would not go to Kunai Valley again—that the two Gides irritated her so much they had her at screaming point. So if a woman was needed, she supposed she was really the only one available.

Yes, that must be it, she decided as she hurriedly packed some clothes and her toilet things. Helen, who was out on the plantation this morning with David, could not very well go, leaving her alone there with David.

At the bedroom door she paused, then turned back and put her armlet in the case with her clothes—as if it were some kind of a talisman. Which, later, it proved to be, oddly enough.

She found Alec standing moodily on the verandah when she appeared with her bag, her sunglasses in her hand. He looked at her disagreeably.

'I appear to have been pushed somewhat into the background. I'd like to know what you've been up to these last few days.'

'Oh, Alec!' Parma felt exasperated. 'You know you don't really care—we might as well give up all this pretence.'

'Might we? It's my bad luck I don't happen to be as available as the planter, is it? Well, I don't want to spoil all your fun, but you won't get anywhere with Pierce. He'll make use of you if it suits him—as it does today—but that will be the end of it. You might observe that he uses Glenda and her brains, but there's no wedding in sight there.'

He had caught her by the arm and she shook off his hand impatiently. 'It's too late to start preaching to me, Alec. Pierce is waiting. I'll have to go. We'll talk later.'

She hurried down the steps, reflecting that once *she* had been the one who wanted to talk, not Alec. She no longer had any illusions about Alec. Marriage had never been in his mind as it had been in hers. It had taken her a long time to recognise that fact, but now it was as plain as daylight.

Pierce swung open the door of the Land-Rover. 'Good girl! Hop in.' His eyes smiled down at her keenly, the gold flecks in them bright in the sunlight.

She didn't ask any questions as they drove through the plantation, and then it was he who spoke first. He didn't apologise for his autocratic interruption of Alec's embrace. He said simply, 'This has given Arthur one hell of a fright. Which in its way may prove to be a good thing.'

'But what's happened, Pierce? If Sophie is ill,

shouldn't Arthur get her to Kundalufa to see a doctor?'

He gave her an oblique look that had the hint of a grim smile in it.

'Sophie has an attack of malaria. But Arthur imagines it's more than just that. He feels guilty that he let the girl try to do a man's work. I don't think she need a doctor, Parma, but when she's over her malaria she'll need to take it easy, and that's for sure.'

'Why does he want you?'

'He needs help—and plenty of it. This business of Sophie is a means of surrendering without losing face. I imagine you understand the set-up—you've heard plenty of talk, and you're not unintelligent.'

She made a wry face. It was not exactly a glowing compliment, but somehow she didn't mind.

'And why do you want me, Pierce?'

'For various reasons. I intend staying at Kunai Valley for a week at least. We'll need someone to look after Sophie and to cope with the cooking as well. Are you tough enough to take it on?'

'Yes, I'm tough enough,' said Parma, rather startled at his choice of that particular word. She had coped with sick girls at Miss Webster's school, and she could cook moderately well. No more was said, but she was still puzzled. 'Various reasons,' he had said—and he had given her only one. And not one word about Alec! Parma thought that *she* would mention Alec.

'Alec was angry with me for coming away like this.'

'Well then, why did you come?' His voice was laconic.

'Because—because I thought it must be urgent.'

'And so it is,' he said equably.

But Parma knew she had not come because of that. She had come because Pierce had asked her. She would go anywhere—anywhere with him. Do anything he told her to do . . .

They went straight in to see Sophie when they

161

reached the Gides' bungalow. She lay shivering under a pile of blankets, her face livid, her nails blue. Arthur looked haggard and drawn, his blond hair falling over his forehead, dark hollows under his eyes. He scarcely acknowledged Parma, but he turned to Pierce desperately.

Pierce said calmly, 'She's been forgetting to take her tablets, has she? Too busy thinking of other things. I hope you haven't been forgetting yours, Arthur.'

'No,' the boy said. 'But I've never had malaria. Sophie used to get it when she was a little kid—it used to upset our mother. Then she had it again when she went over to the coast after Father died. I've given her some tablets—but I've never seen her look as bad as this. Do you think——'

Pierce put a hand on his shoulder. 'She's skin and bone. It always looks worse. She'll be all right. Parma and I will stay for a few days. I'll give you a hand, and Parma will keep an eye on Sophie.' There was a second bed in the disordered room and he tossed Parma a quick glance. 'You'd better sleep in here for tonight, Parma. Have you seen anyone with malaria before?'

'No.'

'Just now she needs to be kept warm. Later she'll be feverish—but that may not be for a few hours yet. She'll want plenty of cold drinks, and she'll need sponging down. Can you manage?'

'Yes. I used to help Matron when the girls at school had fevers.'

'Good. I'll have a little more to say to you presently, but I want to have a talk to Arthur first. Right?'

'Right,' said Parma.

The two men left the room and Parma looked at Sophie, who was moaning softly as she huddled beneath the blankets, her thin body shaking convulsively. She picked up the hot water bottle that had fallen on the floor and went to find the kitchen and fill it up. When she came back to the bedroom, she began to put order into the chaos there—to tidy away clothes and try to make Sophie more comfortable. She had noticed as she came back from the kitchen that the whole bungalow was untidy and dusty, and in the kitchen itself there was a sinkful of dishes.

From somewhere she could hear the murmur of voices as Pierce and Arthur talked, and later she heard the Land-Rover start up and take off. The girl in the bed still lay shivering and Parma felt deep compassion for her. She was such a slight girl, yet she had worked on the plantation at her brother's side. It was no wonder he was so concerned about her now, and so filled with remorse. It was a good thing he had felt able to turn to Pierce, as it seemed there was no one else he could have dealings with.

Parma found sheets in the linen cupboard and made up a bed for herself. She'd have made up a bed for Pierce too, but she didn't know where he intended to sleep. At twelve, *belo* sounded, which meant that work stopped until Monday. Sophie's shivering attack had ended, and now she was burningly hot, her skin dry and flushed. Parma brought her an iced orange drink, and supported her head while she drank it thirstily. Presently she went to the kitchen and prepared a salad from food she found in the refrigerator. From the window she could see the vegetable garden—badly neglected and overgrown with weeds. There was no *hausboi*, that was obvious. And as they had driven up to the bungalow, she had seen no more than a handful of natives working among the coffee trees.

She laid the table in the dining room and was bringing in the plates of salad when she heard the Land-Rover return. Pierce came into the room.

'Oh, you've got lunch. We'll be right in.' He spoke casually and it was certainly not praise, but it pleased Parma somehow to be taken for granted like that. 'How's Sophie?'

She gave him her report and he listened intently.

'I'll just take a look at her before I come in.'

At lunch, Arthur ate very little and scarcely addressed Parma, but then he didn't have much to say to Pierce either.

'We're going back into the trees this afternoon,' Pierce told the girl when they finally got up from the table. 'If anything should worry you—anything at all —there's a car outside in the yard you can use. You'll find us somewhere about the plantation.' His eyes smiled at her, and then he was gone.

Parma cleared the dishes and got the pile of extra washing up out of the way and then went to sit in the bedroom with Sophie. She had already been in to attend to her several times, for she was still burningly hot and parched. Late in the afternoon the fever broke out, and Sophie was saturated with sweat. Parma sponged her, changed her pyjamas and her sheets, and gave her another cold drink. She kept the curtains drawn and felt thankful the bedroom was on the cool side of the house, for the day had been hot. Once evening came, it would cool down.

Towards sundown, Sophie became delirious and began to babble incomprehensibly. Parma sponged her face and neck and her thin arms and murmured to her soothingly, and as she drew up the sheet again there was a burst of coherent words.

'He loves me—he does love me—she shouldn't have come. Oh, Arthur—please, please——' She threw herself about in obvious and acute distress and Parma said gently, 'Don't worry, Sophie—everything's going to be all right.'

For a moment, the blue eyes that had been staring wildly, unseeingly, seemed to focus on Parma's face, and then Sophie threw herself frantically to the other side of the bed. Only a few minutes later she had fallen into an exhausted sleep. Her breathing, heavy at first, slowed down, and the fever subsided. The hectic flush had gone, and the brow was no more than damp.

Parma knew that the worst was over, though Pierce had told her there could be a recurrence of the attack within the next three days.

She smoothed the pillow and sheet, drew up a light blanket, and leaving a small light burning, went quietly out to prepare something for the evening meal. It was almost dark and the air was cool and fresh, and she went into the garden for a few minutes. The glow of sunset was fading from the sky, and the tangle of the uncared-for garden was beautified by the soft fading light. Parma leaned against the trunk of a tall casuarina and thought of what Sophie had said in her delirium. The words troubled her. Who was it who loved Sophie? Was it Pierce? And who was it who shouldn't have come? Somehow, Parma felt that it was herself...

It was not a particularly splendid meal she concocted that night after raiding the vegetable garden for a few beans and carrots. There was no meat in the refrigerator, and she made omelettes with eggs she gathered from the fowlyard. She could certainly not compete with Unkapenna's chicken dishes, but all the same Pierce ate his meal with gusto, and Arthur too was in a better frame of mind. His concern for his sister had been relieved, and Parma knew his mind must be easier about the plantation now that he was able to share his worries.

Everyone went to bed early that night, and the following day, although it was Sunday, the men went down into the trees—to discuss ways and means, Pierce had said. 'We'll want lunch, but we shan't worry you much today, Parma, we'll be talking in the office when we come back.' Sophie was well enough to sit up and eat a little, though she slept a great deal during the day.

'Why are *you* here?' she asked unsmilingly, her blue eyes resentful when, at about eight o'clock, Parma, discovering she was awake, brought her some orange juice and thin toast.

'Because you're sick. I'm here to help.'

'Who asked you?'

'Pierce did. And Arthur asked *him*. So you're not to worry about the plantation,' said Parma cheerfully, sitting down on the side of the bed. Sophie, sipping her orange drink, edged away, making Parma recall how Helen had said she was 'only a child'.

'Our plantation's nothing to do with you. *You* don't care what becomes of us.'

'Of course I do.' Parma, only a year or two older than Sophie, sounded like a tolerant adult humouring a sick child. She held out her hand. 'Here, let me hold that glass while you sit up a bit more. You're going to have orange juice all over yourself.'

Sophie ignored the offer but stared at the hand.

'Why don't you wear that ring on your left hand? Alec gave it to you, didn't he?'

'Yes,' said Parma slowly. She wished she had taken the opal ring off, but the extraordinary fact was that she had forgotten it—just as Pierce had forgotten her drawing. She looked at Sophie's pinched sallow face, the hostile blue eyes, wondering at her obvious dislike, wondering at her question. Was it *Alec* who loved her? And Parma herself who shouldn't have come? She said carefully, 'It's not an engagement ring. I'm not engaged to Alec.'

'I thought that would happen,' Sophie burst out. 'I knew as soon as I saw you that you wouldn't stick to Alec. You think you can steal other people's boyfriends and then drop them and not care who you hurt——'

'But, Sophie——' protested Parma.

The other girl would not let her go on. 'Everything awful that's happened to us is your fault—everything! Alec was in love with me—we'd have been married— he'd have helped run the plantation, and Arthur wouldn't have been sick with worry. They'd never have had that fight. It's all your fault.'

'How can you say that?' Parma interrupted the flood of words indignantly. 'I'd never even heard of you when I met Alec! I certainly didn't steal him from you. And he and your brother had that fight weeks before I came here.'

'But you were coming. Alec told Arthur you were coming—that's why he hadn't been out to see me. You chased him up here. If you'd left him alone he'd have come back to me. I hate you—I hate you! I wish you'd go away.'

CHAPTER ELEVEN

PARMA stood up slowly, and the girl on the bed stared at her, her hatred only too plain in her eyes. It was not good for her to become so upset, but Parma would not have been human if she hadn't been indignant at the unjust accusations that were hurled at her. One would have thought it had been all *her* idea to come here—that Alec had never invited her! And that Alec had no will of his own. If he had dropped Sophie, it was hardly Parma's fault ... But this was no time to argue, and she said with an effort at calmness, 'I'm sorry you feel that way about me. We'll talk about it later. I can't go away just yet—I'm needed here.'

The other girl said nothing in reply. She simply put her empty glass down on the floor and said flatly, 'I'm going to sleep. Go away.'

Her attitude didn't make things easy. Later, while she slept, Parma moved her things out and made up a bed in the next room. She put the opal ring away in her handbag and reflected that she would like to ask Alec a few questions. She was feeling more than a little angry with him. Had he been going to marry Sophie? And had he used Parma as an excuse for breaking it off? It looked as though this was the reason why any schemes of help from him with the plantation had fallen through. Parma thought it was hardly fair that she should get the blame for Alec's inconstancy, and she was thankful that she had fallen out of love with him—even if she had fallen foolishly in love with Pierce!

Three more days went by. Sophie's malaria did not recur, but she was still weak and languid, and she refused to listen to anything that Parma had to say about Alec, simply reasserting stubbornly that she and

Alec had been in love and that Parma had deliberately come between them. However, she made no objection to Parma's setting the house in order, which was a task requiring a great deal of work, for it had been neglected for some time. Parma cleaned floors, dusted, dealt with a large pile of washing that had accumulated, and created order out of the chaos that reigned in the kitchen. As well, she cooked the meals and looked after the everyday needs of Sophie and the two men. At least while she was busy she did not brood over Sophie's poor opinion of her.

Arthur was now very civil and thanked her more than once for looking after his sister and the house. At night, Parma was always tired and retired early and had no chance to talk privately to Pierce. But it gave her pleasure to help him as she was doing, and just to see him every day gave her a great deal of inner happiness. The business of the plantation was never discussed in her hearing, but she knew that they now had a good line-up of workers each morning, and while Pierce was there, the men would keep coming.

Then, when a *hausboi*, Lembang, and his wife Sera were installed in the small cottage behind the bungalow, Parma knew the time had almost come for her to go back to the Barlows. She didn't know if Pierce intended to return to the Butterfly Montane or if he would stay longer at Kunai Valley. As for herself, even though he could not have been kinder or more considerate than he was to her these days, she knew that it must be only because she was proving herself to be of some use. She was quite certain now that she had dreamed that love scene at the *singsing*, and even if it had happened, then it had simply been the result of drinking from the golden gourd ...

The night after Lembang came, she found herself alone with Pierce for the first time. They were sitting in the lamplit sitting room after dinner. The day had been fiercely hot, but now it was raining hard, and the air was restfully cool. Arthur had gone to talk to Sophie who had gone to bed early, and Parma looked across at Pierce, relaxing in one of the shabby old armchairs, and smoking one of his inevitable cigarettes. His eyes glowed darkly in the soft light and his hair had a burnished look. Just to see him there so close made her heart ache a little. He was still very much an enigma. She didn't know what he wanted from her—whether he merely wanted her to be there when she was needed, or whether there was something more to it than that. Neither of them had mentioned Glenda, and she wondered if the Loveday girl was still waiting confidently at the plantation for Pierce to come back.

Pierce looked back at her with a lift of his brows.

'Well, Parma, have you and Sophie been getting on well together?'

The question took her by surprise. 'Not—*very* well,' she admitted ruefully.

'No? How is that? What's the bone of contention?'

Surely he knew! She was certain he must know all about Alec and Sophie.

'I thought you'd have guessed. Alec, of course.'

His eyes searched her face. 'Alec? You're surely not fighting over Alec!'

'Not *fighting*. But Sophie is convinced I stole Alec from her.'

'And you didn't?'

'Well, what do you think?' She flushed with indignation. 'I didn't know anything about Sophie when I met Alec. And even if I had, he's thirty-three, I wouldn't have expected him never to have had a girl-friend before. I'm sorry for Sophie, of course,' she went on, thinking how hopelessly the girl still yearned for Alec. 'Love seems to be—something that just can't be helped. You reach a stage where you can't fight against it, I guess—it's become too much part of your life. We can't all be logical about it, you know,' she concluded, with Glenda in mind.

'Apparently not,' said Pierce. His eyes had hardened. 'It seems it's too much to ask.'

'Is Glenda still at the Butterfly Montane, Pierce?' she asked, following up her line of thought.

'She's gone to friends in Kundalufa,' he said, his voice cold. 'But I don't think you need worry she'll run off with Alec while you're here.'

Parma was quite certain she would not. Glenda was far more interested in Pierce than she was in having a brief love affair with Alec!

Pierce stood up abruptly. 'Well, you'll be needed here a while longer, so make up your mind to that and just try to put up with it, will you? Or is it too much to ask?'

'Not at all,' she said huskily, feeling herself undeservedly rebuffed. He had walked across the room and now his back was to her. His hair needed cutting, it was beginning to curl against his collar and she had an almost uncontrollable desire to touch it. She knew he was tired and wondered if that was making him irritable. There must be something she could say to put him back in a good humour, but before she could think of anything Arthur came into the room and flung himself down on the couch.

'I've been cheering Sophie up—telling her how well everything's going, thanks to you two.'

It was an unusually warm speech from Arthur, and Parma smiled at him sympathetically.

Pierce swung around, scowling. 'There are one or two figures I'd like to go over with you, Arthur.' His eyes flicked to Parma without the glimmer of a smile, and she took the hint and rose.

'If you'll excuse me, I'll go to bed,' she said quietly.

Arthur's goodnight was more friendly than Pierce's, she reflected, and felt badly hurt. What had she done? What had she said?

In her room, she undressed and got into bed, then lay listening to the rain and thinking. Had she been

171

building up groundless hopes while she was here—imagining a sympathy where none existed? Had she been indulging in romantic dreams again without fully admitting it to herself? If she had, then she was crazy. Pierce's attitude to her had softened, but that was all. But his sudden coldness of tonight hurt. How could she be blamed for Sophie's foolish infatuation with Alec? Pierce claimed to have no time for that sort of illogical love, and yet he seemed to be up in arms for Sophie. Meanwhile, Parma was wanted here a little longer—but only because she served a purpose. Not for any other reason in the world....

'You can go back to the Barlows when Pierce comes home this evening,' Sophie said without ceremony after lunch the following day. Lembang was proving to be a good *hausboi*, and Sera a willing gardener and laundress, and Sophie, though she was still listless and satisfied to be waited on, was a hundred per cent improved. 'I can manage without you now. Thank you for your help.' She didn't look at Parma as she said it, and she sounded ungracious, but Parma suspected she was a little ashamed of that very ungraciousness. 'I shan't get out of hand—Arthur says there are plenty of workers on the estate now—for the time being,' she added cynically. 'So I shan't be sitting about the place thinking Arthur is killing himself with worry and overwork and that it's all my fault for letting someone else pinch my boy-friend. At any rate, Pierce will be here a while longer, and I'd much rather you went.' She hovered in the dining room doorway, and her face was very young and childish.

'Very well,' said Parma, troubled. Pierce would simply have to concede and let her go. 'I'm only sorry you feel as you do about me and Alec. I wish there was something I could do to convince you that—that you'd be better to forget him. It's *over*, Sophie—can't you see that?'

Tears had flown to the other girl's eyes. 'No, I can't see it. Before you interfered, it was wonderful. Now Alec won't come here because Arthur told him to keep away or he'd—he'd—— And he's the only man I'll ever love—ever, ever!' Tears ran down her face and she put her fists to her eyes in a childish gesture and turning away blindly ran to her room. Parma heard the bed move as she threw herself on to it. Sophie had certainly cast her in the role of scapegoat! And yet what were the facts? Arthur had taken a swing at Alec —wasn't that how Alec had put it?—because the Didirman had dropped his sister for another girl. (Though Sophie preferred to put it another way.) In any case, Alec had then backed out of giving the expected help at Kunai Valley. The fight certainly couldn't have improved relations, and in Sophie's view it was all Parma's fault!

It was hopeless. Parma sighed and rather slowly went to her room. If she was to go, then she had better pack her things, strip off her bed, and leave the room in order. Nobody really wanted her at Kunai Valley. She had been foolishly happy because she had thought she was being of service to Pierce. Parma discovered there were tears in her eyes too. She opened the top drawer of the chest, and there was the armlet that the old *luluai* had given her. She took it up and looked lovingly at the blue-green pattern made by the beetle shells, gently stroked the soft feathers. *Gras bilong kumul.* Absently she fastened it on her arm. She would have to give it to Helen Barlow when she left the country. She thought of the *singsing* and of how happy she had been, and of the dreamed or remembered kiss. It was a painful business—to love and not to be loved— to spend your life chasing butterflies.

Through the window she could see the Gides' shabby car standing under its shelter beyond the garden, and as she stood musing it occurred to her that there was one thing she could do to help Sophie before she left. She wasn't sure if it would lead to happiness or to disaster, but at least it would resolve Sophie's dilemma.

She would go to Varmari to fetch Alec.

And perhaps, she thought wistfully, perhaps Sophie would prove to be right, perhaps Alec really did love her. Arthur would forgive him, he and Sophie would be married, Alec would help with the plantation, and they at least would live happily ever after . . .

She went to the door of Sophie's room. The girl was lying with one arm flung across her face and she appeared to be asleep. Parma hesitated, then she went through to the back of the house, and stepped out into the garden.

'Lembang!'

The *hausboi* appeared in a few seconds from the vegetable garden.

'Misis?'

'*Mi go long Varmari. Yu tokim Misis longtaim i gerap. Yu savvy?*'

'*Mi savvy.*'

Parma was satisfied. Lembang would tell Sophie where she had gone, though he would not be able to tell her why.

A few minutes later she got into the car and checked the petrol, checked too that there was a spare can in the boot as Helen had taught her to do. She hoped that she would not see Pierce as she drove down the road through the trees, and then she was disappointed when she did not. Because even to see him in the distance gave her a painful pleasure—and was better than not to see him at all. The day was dull and cloudy as if in tune with her mood, and the ground was still wet after last night's rain, and Parma started off confidently towards Varmari.

She wasn't really as sure of the way as she had imagined she would be. She had to watch out for a side road, and they were often half hidden by the dense jungle growth so that you could pass a turn off without ever seeing it. Then of course you had to be sure you took the right one. Parma passed three side roads without recognising them, and then she drove for miles without catching sight of another track. She began to fear she had missed the way when she saw a great clump of bamboo that she remembered, and on the far side of it was an opening. She made the turn quickly, and began to drive upwards through steep hills. She was quite certain she had been this way before and began to feel more sure of herself, and to imagine what would happen when she reached the Government Station. If Alec was not in, she would leave a message for him to come to Kunai Valley. She was pretty certain he would come—if only to find out the reason she wanted him. That way, she could get herself back over the worst of the road before it got really dark. Beyond that she didn't think. Alec and Sophie would meet again and they would have to settle things their own way. As for herself, she didn't want to think of Pierce taking her back to the Butterfly Montane—and of the farewells that she knew must lie at the end of it.

Her thoughts were interrupted by a long roll of thunder, and in a minute there was a cloudburst. The road, narrow and winding, was already very difficult to drive on, and it was taking her longer to reach Varmari than she had imagined it would. She negotiated a wide bend and the road ahead sloped steeply downwards. At the bottom of it she could see the waters of a small stream. It was by no means unusual for roads to cross creek beds, and she was not worried. The water, as she approached it, looked not more than a couple of inches deep, but she slowed down and approached it gently. Beyond, she could see the rise of the road, and she felt optimistically certain that once she reached the top of the rise she would be able to see the mission school, and from there it was no distance to Varmari.

She heard the splash of water as she drove the car into the stream. The water seemed much deeper than she had expected, and she didn't know whether to put her foot on the accelerator or to creep along. By the time she had decided she had better accelerate, it was too late. The engine had stalled, the car had stopped dead, and she couldn't get it going again. The rain was now pelting down smartly, so that the jungle ahead and behind was little more than a white sheet. Parma sat dismayed, not knowing what to do. She remembered that other time when she had been in difficulties and the crowd of natives had come running towards her in their fierce-looking get-ups. How frightened she had been then! It would be altogether different now, but she couldn't see any sign of any rescue party.

Once the downpour had stopped, she thought she would leave the car and climb the road ahead, and see if she was right about the mission school. If so, then her troubles would be at an end. If not—well, she would face that eventuality when, and if, it came. Meanwhile, she sat and waited, and although the rain eased off the white blanket seemed to become thicker. It must be something to do with condensation, she decided. She looked at her watch, but it had stopped, and she had no idea at all of the time.

Some time later the rain stopped altogether. Parma removed her sandals and, carrying them, climbed from the car. The water had grown deeper and reached almost up to her knees. It was running fast and she had to move with care, for the stream bed was stony and treacherous. On the other side, she wiped some of the water from her feet with her handkerchief and fastening on her sandals again, began the long climb up the hill. She would have been thankful to see anyone at all—a native with a pig and a boar's tusk through his nose, a woman with a load of firewood, a child from the mission school—but she saw nobody. It was as though there were nobody in this part of the world but herself. And when she reached the top of the long steep rise and looked about her, there was no mission school, nothing at all but dense jungle pressing in, and ever-rising mountains hidden in white mists.

And the end of the road. A road to nowhere.

In her heart, Parma knew already that she had taken the wrong turning. This only confirmed it. But if there was a road as far as this, there must be a village somewhere about and she was going to find it. She *had* to find it. She wished now that she had worn shoes instead of sandals, but determinedly she began to push her way through thick undergrowth.

She didn't know how far she went, but it was all jungle, there was not a clearing, not a sign of habitation of any sort. By now, there was nothing to do but go on—and on and on, until she finally found a village or a garden. If she turned back, she doubted very much whether she would be able to find the car again.

It was getting towards sundown now. The clouds were low and heavy and the world was becoming grey and silent. At least it wasn't raining. Parma pressed on, a fear that she would not admit to in her heart. It was dark when, after taking a downward slope, she reached a gorge that was crossed by a long swaying bridge. Varmari! This was the bridge she had crossed with Pierce—and she was at the far side of it! Once she had made her way over it, she would soon find the Government Station. If the worst came to the worst, she could start shouting. Someone would hear her— the dogs would hear her and start barking. Alec would come through the dark and find her...

She started across the bridge and it swung and swayed. The moon appeared fitfully from behind clouds, disappeared again so that the darkness seemed darker than ever. Parma clung to the bush vines that supported the bridge, took each step with trembling care on the horrifyingly narrow footway. The saplings were slippery and so were her sandals, and the bridge seemed endlessly long. Now a wind had begun to blow, the clouds scudded, and the moonlight made weird dizzying shadows in the gorge below.

Why did the bridge sway so sickeningly? Was it the wind? Or was there someone behind her? Parma dared not look back into the moon-patched darkness behind her for fear of what she might see. She tried to call out, but when her voice came—'Who's there?'—it was little more than a husky whisper. There was no answer but the sound of the river that rushed and tumbled in the darkness far below.

When she reached the end of the bridge, it was suddenly pitch dark and she could not make herself look back. It was not the bridge at Varmari—it was half as long again. But she began to stumble forward among the trees hurrying, hurrying, knowing that there must be a path—there must be people—somewhere, somewhere. But how, in this pitching dizzying darkness, could she find a path? She slipped—clutched at ferns, at tough, foot-long leaves, while all around her shadows looped and swung as the moonlight came snaking and twisting among the trees.

Now, muffled and low, she could hear the beat of kundu drums. Or was it the sound of footsteps? She tried to run, but the shadows had been joined in ghostly partnership by white swirling mists, and the ground was slippery with fallen leaves and water. Ahead Parma saw—or thought she saw—a great dark form lumbering among the trees—snuffling at ferns and mosses, blotting out the way——

The devil-pig!

Parma lost her head entirely and in a nightmare panic charged blindly to one side. She was nowhere near Varmari—she was in the cloud forest! Her feet slipped and then she tripped over a giant root—her arms flew out wildly and she was falling—falling——

She knew nothing more until she opened her eyes to

find herself in a native hut. A primitive lamp lit up the room where she lay on a thick mat on a floor of bamboo canes. Her sodden dress was spread out near by, and her body was draped in a cloth of woven fibres, decorated by a strange native design.

Dark smiling faces peered down at her—girls in grass aprons with red flowers in their hair and strings of beads and shells hanging down over naked breasts. Parma put her hand to her forehead and felt a swelling where she must have struck her head when she fell. Her head ached dully, and the girls were speaking to her excitedly, but she could not understand a word.

'*Mi wi?*' she asked. 'Where am I?' They looked at her and giggled. '*Mi laik i go long* Varmari.'

Still they stared. Then one of them—a young girl with a dark gleaming skin—reached down and touched her arm, and Parma remembered she was still wearing her armlet.

'Masta Adams,' the girl said, and the others repeated the words eagerly. 'Masta Adams!'

Masta Adams. Parma leaned back weakly on her hands. How she wished that Masta Adams were here! It struck her as significant that the shining girl connected her armlet with Pierce's name, and it seemed very possible that these might be some of the villagers who had been at the *singsing*. But they didn't understand pidgin—not her pidgin, at any rate—and they didn't seem to speak it. Presently one of them, who had left the hut, came back with a banana leaf on which were two flat brown cakes. They were offered to Parma with a wide friendly smile that showed beautiful teeth. Because it was expected of her, she began to eat one of the cakes, and found it not unpleasant. She thought it was made from a mixture of *kaukau* and the small unsweet bananas that were prevalent in the Highlands.

'*Gutpela kaikai,*' she said with a smile, when she had managed to demolish both of the cakes. Strangely, her

179

head did not ache so much now, and slowly she got to her feet, while the girls watched with evident approval. The cloth that was draped about her fell to just below the knee and was fastened securely on one shoulder with a fibre string. Her slender legs and arms looked very white beside all the gleaming dark flesh around her. Parma wished she could communicate in some way, but the only thing they seemed able to say to her, or she to them, that embraced the outside world at all, consisted of the two words, Masta Adams.

Parma repeated them now, and it was strangely comforting. 'Masta Adams *i wi*?' But they either did not understand or they could not tell her where Pierce was. They simply stood around her and smiled and smiled. And then, as she stood wondering what on earth she was to do next, they began gently to urge her out of the hut. Beyond the doorway, flowers were growing, and one of the girls pulled a red hibiscus and laughingly fastened it in Parma's hair. They danced about her as they led her across an open space towards a longer hut from which a light glowed dimly. There they pushed her inside and left her.

Parma found herself confronted by the old *luluai* who had given her the armband. She could have wept with relief as she recalled that he understood a little English.

He looked at her gravely. He sat cross-legged in the lamplit hut, on a low seat that was covered with a mat of woven palm leaves. On the wall behind him was a beautiful *tapa*, boldly decorated in red and black. The *luluai* looked infinitely impressive and noble, and Parma knew that this was something to do with his essential being, for tonight he wore no splendid feathered headdress. He was bare-footed, there was a simple beaded band around his brow, and a large shining kinya shell hung against his breast. Otherwise, he wore only a laplap.

'You sit,' he told the girl, with quiet gravity, and

Parma sat beside him on the seat. Her heart was beating fast, but she was not in the least afraid. The *luluai* reached for a thick bamboo container, with figures carved upon it, and she said carefully and slowly, 'It was kind of the girls to take care of me. I am lost.'

The ancient chief touched the feathers of her armband, and the ghost of a smile came into his dark old eyes and vanished again.

'Masta Adams,' he said.

He passed her a greenish nut which she recognised as *buai*—betel nut—and he took one himself. Something Helen had once told her flashed through her mind—In certain villages, if you were not offered *buai*, it was a sign that you were to be killed.

'Well, at least I'm not going to be killed,' thought Parma. She felt a little lightheaded, and she wanted to laugh at her thought. Because that sort of thing did not happen now—except perhaps in areas that were still prohibited to Europeans. And it was quite ridiculous to think of this noble headman killing a young English girl ... She watched him tear off the outside of the nut with his teeth, and she did the same. Inside, the nut was pink, and Parma bit off a small piece. The *luluai* passed her a golden yellow gourd that had a carved stick in it, and she knew that it contained lime and she took a tiny amount and put it in her mouth with the *buai*. The *buai* had a slightly bitter, astringent taste, and the lime burned a little. Now there must be a red juice in her mouth as there was in the *luluai*'s, and soon she would have to spit—as he was doing.

With great courtesy, he handed her some green pepper leaf, and rather thankfully she chewed that. She hoped she would not have to sample any more of the *buai*, but she was determined that he should not know how little she liked it.

She said, slowly, 'I would like to go to Masta Adams.'

The *luluai* nodded, then turned his head slightly. Parma's eyes followed his—across the hut to the low door giving on to the darkness of the night. There— just inside—in the flickering lamplight, she saw Pierce Adams standing—tall, arms folded, eyes glinting with amusement as he looked back at her.

'So you want to go to Masta Adams, do you, Parma?'

She could do nothing but stare, as her heart began to beat in great slow thuds like the pulse of the kundu drum.

CHAPTER TWELVE

HE sat down with them after that, and accepted *buai*, and he and the *luluai* talked. They talked about Parma who had been found 'asleep' in the forest. They had known she 'belonged' to Master Adams by the band on her arm. 'So we send for you.' It was quite crazy, and Parma, sitting at the *luluai*'s side, found it hard to believe any of it. The most incredible thing of all was that Pierce should be there—passing the lime gourd, accepting a pepper leaf, and occasionally looking at Parma as gravely as the *luluai* did. She could not keep her eyes off him. Tonight he wore light-coloured trousers and a cream woollen sweater with a high neck, and his skin looked a dark golden brown. Gold lights gleamed in his hair, but his eyes were shadowed and dark, and she was not always certain whether he was looking at her or not.

At last he thanked the *luluai* for his kindness and rose to his feet.

'Come, Parma, it's time for us to go.'

She slipped to her feet and was immediately aware of her strange dress, of the flower in her hair, and of the fact that Pierce from his height was looking down at her with deep concentration. What was he thinking? That it was absurd for her, a non-Territorian, to be decked out like this? There was certainly the suspicion of a smile on his lips.

A few minutes later they left the village together. Some of the villagers came from their huts to see them go, and Parma waved and smiled and called her thanks. Pierce, who had a powerful torch, kept hold of her arm as they walked through the mist-wreathed forest. They didn't go across the swaying bridge, and it seemed no distance at all to the jeep-track and Pierce's

Land-Rover. Once there, he hustled her into the car without ceremony and she felt the flower slip from her hair. He reached into the back and produced a woollen stole—it belonged to Sophie, no doubt—and handed it to her.

'Put that around yourself. You're shivering.'

When he was seated beside her, he turned sideways and looked hard at her, first flicking on his torch, but not directing the beam at her.

'So you thought you were going to Varmari, did you? What in hell for? Would you tell me that? I thought I told you you were to stay at Kunai Valley.'

'Sophie said I must leave. And I wanted to find Alec,' said Parma. Her teeth were chattering, but it was not entirely from the cold.

'Are you as infatuated as all that? For God's sake, haven't your eyes been opened yet? Romantic love is all very well, and I don't doubt you would live at Varmari quite happily if it suited you—you've proved your adaptability to me in many ways.' He sounded impatient, and his eyes, half amused, half grim, raked over her get-up, now partly hidden by the stole, and lingered on the red stain at one corner of her mouth. 'But you deserve better than Alec Rivers, and if I hadn't been so tied up at Kunai Valley for the last little while I'd have proved it to you quite forcefully, I promise you. You talked enough nonsense last night to turn my hair white! And then what must you do but go running off to Alec Rivers to get him to take you away.'

'I *didn't*,' said Parma, who had been listening stupefied. A sudden jerk at the torch sent the light blindingly into her eyes, and she automatically reached out only to have her wrist taken and to find herself pulled with savage forcefulness against Pierce's body. The torch went out, and his mouth was on hers, and in a second she felt herself relaxing into his kiss, surrendering completely. Sophie's stole slipped from her bare shoulder, and his hand was there, warm, caressing...

His voice was tense when he released her. 'Does that prove anything to you, Parma Drew?'

From her own angle, it proved nothing that she did not know—she loved him passionately and for ever. As far as he was concerned, she would have liked to think it proved a lot of things, but she dared take nothing for granted, though her heart was thudding madly. He flicked on the torch and turned it mercilessly on her face.

'Look at me now and try to convince me you've reached the stage where you can't fight against your feelings for the Didirman——'

'Don't,' she said huskily. Somewhere beyond that blinding light he was staring into her face and reading all that was written there, and she couldn't look back at him—couldn't see what *his* eyes betrayed. Now he turned off the torch again and lit the dashboard light and in its soft glow she looked fully at the face that she knew by heart—at the curve of lips where she longed to trace a finger, at eyes that were—surely—tender, as well as questioning.

'If you'd *listen* to me, Pierce,' she said.

'Yes? I'm listening. But I don't want to hear any more rubbish about Alec Rivers being part of your life——'

'You're not going to. I was talking about Sophie when I said that. I was trying to get Alec to go back to *Sophie*, because I think she may be the girl he really loves. Don't you see?'

'And that's a lot of nonsense too,' said Pierce. 'But it's nonsense I don't mind hearing. Now come here.' He reached out and drew Parma back against his warm body. 'Let's have that again. Are you telling me you're willing to nobly sacrifice your love for Alec for Sophie's sake? Or are you telling me something else?'

'I'm telling you something else,' she said huskily. She was looking unwaveringly into his eyes and he was looking steadily back at her and it was like heaven.

'Such as that you've come to your senses? Such as that you really meant it when you told the *luluai* you wanted to go to Masta Adams?'

'Yes,' breathed Parma, almost fearfully. And remembered something that she should never have forgotten. Glenda Loveday. She felt her heart die within her breast. 'But of course I know that you and Glenda——'

'Have been friends since childhood, and beyond that there's nothing to know,' he said briefly. 'Why do you think I had the *luluai* give *you* that love potion at the *singing* the other night?'

Parma gasped, laughing a little. So it had been a love potion! 'Then you did kiss me! I thought it was a dream.'

'I did kiss you, Parma Drew. It was no dream.'

'I thought you hated me because of that other girl—Rowena Arnold. Because I reminded you of her, and she'd broken your heart.'

His dark eyebrows went up. 'All hearts must be broken at least once. I imagine even you, young though you are, know that.'

She nodded, and William Cunningham flitted like the merest shadow through her mind.

'You reminded me of Rowena only at first—and only superficially. Because you were a girl who'd come out here with a lot of romantic notions about love, and you were bound to find the whole thing sooner or later turn to dust and ashes in your hands.'

'Like my little palm basket?'

'Yes, just like that. And I'd have preferred to see you disillusioned by the country rather than by the man. It's less hurtful. But you weren't so easily frightened away as I imagined you'd be.' He laughed a little. 'And then I was mad enough to fall in love with you myself.'

Parma looked at him in wondering amazement. But his arm was close about her, and it was all true.

'I fought it, of course. But you tempted me too often —and I gave in to temptation too often. There must have been times when you thought me little more than a savage. I had to keep reminding myself that your kind of girl was trouble, that the best thing that could happen for all of us was for you to——'

'Pack up and go? That was why you took me to Varmari, wasn't it? To show me that the place was too tough for me.'

'Yes. I thought it would work, and I steeled myself every day to hear you were off. Then you said your brave little piece about not being so stupid that you couldn't adapt to the needs of the man you loved. Do you remember?'

She nodded, colouring deeply.

'That was when I gave in—to you, but not to Alec. I was vain enough to consider myself a better proposition than Alec. It was unethical perhaps, but by then I was too deeply committed to care. I even resorted to love potions! Is that sufficiently romantic for you, my dearest girl?'

'Yes,' she said with a deep sigh.

'And do you know that I love you madly and feverishly and for ever?'

'Yes.'

'Then come closer.'

It was some time before either of them spoke again, and then Parma freed herself a little to ask, 'Do you think we can get Alec to go back to Sophie, Pierce? She's so terribly much in love——'

'Now you're being too romantic by half, my girl. Sophie is young—she'll survive and be the better for it. If she and Arthur had lived in the district a little longer, and mixed around a bit more, they'd have known all about Alec and his girl-friends, and Sophie would never have fallen in love with him. No, there's to be no interfering there. The Gides will be all right. I'm making Arthur a loan—but that's between you

187

and me, I don't want it to go any further. So now let's forget about everyone else.' He touched her feathered armlet. 'You'll be able to keep that for ever now, Parma Drew, because you're going to marry a coffee planter.'

She looked at him with a smile that was a little mischievous, though her heart was beating fast with happiness. 'Do you think—do you think I'll adapt, Pierce?'

'Darling, I think you *have* adapted. When I saw you accepting that *buai*, my very last doubt went. You're a Territorian, my little Parma. *Yu bilong tiru.*'

A Treasury of Harlequin Romances!

Many of the all time favorite Harlequin Romance Novels have not been available, until now, since the original printing. But on this special introductory offer, they are yours in an exquisitely bound, rich gold hardcover with royal blue imprint. Three complete unabridged novels in each volume. And the cost is so very low you'll be amazed!

This very special collection of classic Harlequin Romances would be a distinctive addition to your library. And imagine what a delightful gift they'd make for any Harlequin reader!

Start your collection now. See reverse of this page for **SPECIAL INTRODUCTORY OFFER!**

V

FREE!

Harlequin Romance Catalogue

Here is a wonderful opportunity to read many of the Harlequin Romances you may have missed.

The HARLEQUIN ROMANCE CATALOGUE lists hundreds of titles which possibly are no longer available at your local bookseller. To receive your copy, just fill out the coupon below, mail it to us, and we'll rush your catalogue to you!

Following this page you'll find a sampling of a few of the Harlequin Romances listed in the catalogue. Should you wish to order any of these immediately, kindly check the titles desired and mail with coupon.

To: HARLEQUIN READER SERVICE, Dept. N 306
M.P.O. Box 707, Niagara Falls, N.Y. 14302
Canadian address: Stratford, Ont., Canada

☐ Please send me the free Harlequin Romance Catalogue.

☐ Please send me the titles checked.

I enclose $_____ (No C.O.D.'s), All books are 60c each. To help defray postage and handling cost, please add 25c.

Name _____

Address _____

City/Town _____

State/Prov. _____ Zip_____

Have You Missed Any of These
Harlequin Romances?

All books are 60c. Please use the handy order coupon.

BB